D0928754

THE SECRET OF
BENJAMIN SQUARE

When a stranger calls at their New England farmhouse to inform Nancy and her brother Robert that they are the heirs of a British nobleman, and that a fortune can be theirs if they agree to move to the ancestral home of Benjamin House in London, it seems like all their childhood dreams have come true. But upon arrival, Nancy is soon homesick — while Robert nearly loses his life in an 'accident'. Then there's the mysterious ancient riddle connected with the house that could point the way to hidden treasure . . .

Books by Michael Kurland
in the Linford Mystery Library:

THE TRIALS OF QUINTILIAN
VICTORIAN VILLAINY
THE INFERNAL DEVICE
DEATH BY GASLIGHT
MISSION: THIRD FORCE
MISSION: TANK WAR
A PLAGUE OF SPIES

MICHAEL KURLAND

◆

THE SECRET OF BENJAMIN SQUARE

Complete and Unabridged

LINFORD
Leicester

First published in Great Britain

First Linford Edition
published 2017

A catalogue record for this book is available
from the British Library.

ISBN 978–1–4448–3347–8

Published by
F. A. Thorpe (Publishing)
Anstey, Leicestershire

Set by Words & Graphics Ltd.
Anstey, Leicestershire
Printed and bound in Great Britain by
T. J. International Ltd., Padstow, Cornwall

This book is printed on acid-free paper

Face Second Watch from Benjamin
	Square
Pace out the steps, for you know
	what is there
Left march when you come about
	the great ring
Out, up, to the left, and return
	to the King.

1

The rain was an incessant droning on the carriage roof, punctuated by the chop-chop of the horse's iron shoes on the wet cobblestones and the random creaking of leather against wood. The driver, great-coat buttoned to his neck, stood in his perch, with his back against the great piles of baggage strapped to the roof, and guided the horse through the narrow, potholed, garbage-littered London streets. He swore in an unimaginative steady mono-tone as the carriage lurched and jerked and the rain worked its way under his collar and down his back.

Inside the coach four people sat, one in each corner, staring at each other. The three men were carrying on a desultory conversation, ignoring the cold, damp wind that whipped through the cracks and the erratic jouncing of their leather seats. The fourth passenger, a slender woman barely into her twenties, was huddled on the seat, her legs under her, traveling cloak about her and the coach blanket over all. She was cold, and frightened, homesick and miserable, and had about reached the point where she didn't care if anyone else could tell or not. Another five minutes . . . another minute . . . sometime in the next thirty seconds she would break down and start crying.

The man sitting next to her, a dark man with the same regularity of features that made them both handsome, looked over and saw her distress. He reached out and put his arm around her, pulling her over until her head rested on his broad shoulder. 'Nancy,' he said, 'oh, Nancy. This isn't easy for you, any of it. And it starts out by being cold and rainy, like a bad omen.'

The man across from Nancy struck a sulphurous match, filling the coach with its smell, and puffed away at an ancient briar. 'Beg your pardon, Mister Hooker — or should I say Lord Benjamin? — Beg your pardon, milord, but you can't count the weather as an omen. Whenever you come to London you stand a better than even chance of finding the weather just like this. Sometimes it's worse, if it comes to that.'

'Worse?' Robert Hooker smiled. 'Tell me, Sir Andrew, how could it get worse than it is right now?'

'Fog, sir. The famous London pea-soup fog. Can't see your hand in front of your face. I remember once back in the winter of sixty-four — February it was, and that would make it sixty-five — when I was walking through the old Regent Circus . . . ' Sir Andrew Dean launched comfortably into another of his inexhaustible supply of anecdotes, sending little puffy smoke rings into the air in front of him as he spoke.

Nancy snuggled against her brother's shoulder and allowed her thoughts to wheel free, trying to envisage what this new life she was entering would be like. Images of a horde of curtseying maids and bowing butlers crossed her mind, all carrying large silver trays and saying, 'Yes, Lady Nancy; of course, Lady Nancy.' Then they faded away, to be replaced by a

3

small group of aristocratic British women who were standing around her in their proper white gowns and murmuring, 'After all, she *is* an American; I suppose one *must* make allowances,' in that cultured British accent she could never hope to duplicate. 'We had her to tea last week, and you'll never *guess* which spoon she used for the sugar!' they'd say, giggling behind their fans. Nancy pulled the collar of her coat higher around her neck and wished she were home.

'So,' Robert said, 'my correct title is Lord Benjamin? Not Lord Hooker?'

'That is so,' Sir Andrew told him. 'You are Robert Hooker, Lord Benjamin, not Lord Robert or Lord Hooker. And Miss Nancy, as your sister, is The Honorable Miss Nancy Hooker.'

'Not Lady Nancy?'

'No, milord. That distinction will be reserved for your wife, when you marry.'

'Ah!' said Robert.

Well, Nancy thought, *that's good. I don't know if I could get used to being called Lady anything.*

'I have instructed the servants to have the fires laid on in the great room and all the bedrooms you'll be using,' the third man, Doctor Moran, said in his dry voice. 'I believe you'll be comfortable once you get inside and out of the chill. I think I shall prescribe a cup of hot cocoa for you, Miss Nancy.'

'Thank you, Doctor,' she said.

Robert peered through the small window, trying to make out some details of the streets they were passing through. 'So this is the City of London,' he said. 'And I thought Boston was large.'

'Well, sir,' Sir Andrew said, 'it's not exactly — not legally, as you might say — the City of London. We've already passed through that. This is the Unincorporated Borough of Marylebone.'

'Marylebone?'

'Spelled to be pronounced Mary-le-bone: bad French for Mary the Good. An old name. This is Marylebone Road we're on now. We turn off onto Benjamin Road in a few moments. Then it's only a few minutes to Benjamin Square and Benjamin House, your new home.'

'I thought we lived in London,' Nancy said.

'You shall soon enough if the council-men have their way. They're trying to incorporate all the surrounding boroughs into a sort of 'Greater London.' Probably will too; it makes sense.'

The brougham wheeled around a corner to the right and proceeded cautiously up the street. Nancy could make out a row of two-story villas, each with a fronting miniature garden, and identical even to the fencing at the pavement. They gave way to a block of respectable Georgian town houses.

'A bad introduction to your city, I'll grant you,' Sir Andrew said. 'It could have been one of our rare sunny days.'

'My city?' Nancy's attention was brought back inside the carriage. 'Yes, it is my city now, isn't it?'

Sir Andrew laughed. 'As soon as the beaux of London society are introduced to you, I'm sure the city will be yours heart and soul.'

Nancy felt herself blushing. 'I didn't mean it that way at all,' she protested. 'It's just that this is my home now.'

'Speaking of home,' Sir Andrew said, 'we're just about there. Benjamin Square is right ahead of us.'

Nancy peered out of the window. The street ahead came to a Y-shaped intersection with two others, and three straight rows of fences marked off a large center green.

'It's been misnamed,' Nancy said as the carriage swung into the intersection. 'It should be called Benjamin Triangle.'

'Which is Benjamin House?' Robert asked.

'Dead ahead,' Sir Andrew said, pointing. 'The house on the left.'

Nancy stared at the huge edifice of ancient stone. It was three stories high and as solid-looking as the Great Pyramid. Two square stone columns went up, one on each side of the great barred doors, and terminated in towers above the gabled roof.

'It *has* been misnamed,' Robert said with a rare smile. 'It should have been called Benjamin Castle.'

'It was built several hundred years ago

as a manor house near London,' Sir Andrew told Robert, 'and in the course of time London has expanded to meet it. When it was built, there was good cause to make it defendable as a prime architectural consideration.'

In a window on the third floor of the great house a curtain was thrust aside, and a tanned face looked down at the approaching brougham. In a second it was joined by another face: a massive, brutal face with the thick ears and lips of the professional plug-ugly.

'Is't them, Sor?'

The owner of the tanned face, a handsome young man with an air of authority and control, ducked his head in and closed the curtain slightly to assure that he would not be seen. 'Aye, Bill, 'tis them indeed.' He kept watching as the carriage stopped at the steps and its passengers climbed down. 'There's Sir Andrew out first . . . and that must be Robert Hooker, our American lord . . . and Doctor Moran . . . ah! Nancy Hooker, his new lordship's sister. Quite a good-looking woman appears to be bundled under that thick cloak. We must see that she likes it here, eh, Bill?'

'Indeed, Sor, indeed,' the plug-ugly agreed with a wide smile on his thick lips.

As Nancy reached the archway formed by the two stone columns far overhead, she looked up at the massive stonework about her. There were small stone figures peering around corners and out of cracks, and staring evilly down at the party below. For a moment she had the impression that the very stones of the house had assumed malignant shapes to frighten her away, to tell her she wasn't wanted here. Then she realized they were only stone carvings, as ancient as the house itself, crouching through the centuries on the narrow ledge.

'Look, Robert,' she said, pointing up at the grinning monstrosities. 'Gargoyles!'

'Not gargoyles,' Sir Andrew said, coming up behind her. 'Merely basilisks and other imaginary stone monsters.'

'You mean it isn't a gargoyle unless it's hung from a church?'

'Not that at all,' Sir Andrew explained. 'It isn't a gargoyle unless it has a drainpipe coming out of its mouth to empty on unsuspecting passers-by below. There are gargoyles on the corners of the roof, but the beasties above you are just stone statues.'

'Oh,' Nancy said. Her eye was suddenly attracted to a movement of the drapes in one of the third-floor windows. She saw a head at the window, but it pulled back before she could make out what it looked like. A second face remained at the window, staring down on the little group below. It was a face as repulsive as any of the stone figures crouched on the ledge below it. Nancy gave an involuntary gasp and put her hand to her face.

'What is it?' Robert asked.

'That man — in the window. Who is he?'

Robert and Sir Andrew looked up, but by the time they could tell which window Nancy was referring to, the face had withdrawn from view.

'One of the servants, perhaps,' Sir Andrew said reassuringly.

'He startled me,' Nancy said, choosing not to comment on the horrible ugliness of the face she had seen.

Doctor Moran hurried up the steps and pulled the bell-pull. He was dwarfed by the great wooden doors, which were heavily barred and studded with large iron bolt-heads. In a second they swung open, and a liveried servant stared suspiciously at them, then gave a half-bow and stood respectfully aside. 'Doctor Moran,' he said. 'Sir Andrew. And this must be our new master.'

'That's right, Piggins,' Doctor Moran said, stepping inside. 'And I hope that — ' The sentence was never finished; there was a rumbling noise above them, and Nancy looked up just in time to see a large square stone hurtling downward from the arch high above.

'Robert!' she screamed.

He had no time to react. The stone hit the ground beside him, shattering into a thousand fragments that scattered across the area like shards from an exploding bomb. When the dust cleared, Robert was lying on the steps, a pool of blood widening around him and dripping slowly down the stone stairway.

2

Doctor Moran knelt by Robert and examined him briefly. 'He's alive,' he said. 'Unconscious, but alive. Help me get him upstairs.'

Sir Andrew took Robert's feet, and the two of them bundled him inside and quickly carried the motionless form to an upstairs bedroom. Nancy slowly followed them upstairs, stopping outside the door. She couldn't grasp what had just happened: it was unreal, like a scene in a play. Any second the act would be over. Any second her brother Robert would get out of the bed, wipe off the blood — stage blood, not his life's blood that had dripped on the staircase and spurted into her hand as she had tried to help lift him — and tell her that the act was over, and he was all right, and this was all some kind of joke, and he was sorry he frightened her. Any second.

But the seconds passed, and Doctor

Moran left the room looking worried, his hands covered with blood. Nancy went to the door and looked in, and there was her brother on the bed, his clothes cut away, his body looking pale against the newly scarlet sheet. Sir Andrew was standing at the foot of the bed, tearing a clean sheet into long thin strips.

'May I help?' Nancy asked, finding her voice at last.

Sir Andrew handed her a sheet. 'I'm sorry, my dear. I'm so sorry. What a horrible thing. Can't think how it could have happened. That stone's been there two hundred years. What a horrible thing for you.'

'Yes,' Nancy said. 'It's worse for Robert. How is he, can you tell?'

'That's Doctor Moran's field, not mine. He seems hopeful — strong pulse and all that. Went downstairs to get his black bag. Doctors can't do a thing without their black bags. Says we caught the bleeding in time — that's the main thing. Have to wait to see about possible skull fractures, things like that.'

'Oh!' Nancy's fist went to her mouth as

she pictured Robert paralyzed or turned into a mindless vegetable by the crushing blow on his head.

'There — now I've frightened you, and with no cause. I am sorry. Doctor Moran says there's no external sign of anything like that; we just have to wait to be sure.'

'Here, now; what's this?' Doctor Moran appeared in the doorway, his dark eyes staring intently at Nancy. 'Let's have none of this, young lady. Your brother will be fine; you just let us worry about him. Here — you take this in a glass of water and lie down. Meb! Show Miss Nancy to her bedroom and lay the bed for her, or whatever it is you do. Take care of her.' He handed Nancy a twist of paper full of white powder and pushed her gruffly out of the room.

'This way, miss,' the young serving-woman said, and led Nancy down the hall to a bedroom. 'There's a pitcher of water and a glass on the bureau. The fire's laid and the bed's made. I am very sorry, miss. Here, let me.'

Meb poured a glass of water, stirred the powder in, and handed it to Nancy. It tasted slightly bitter, but she drank it down without protest and handed the glass back. 'Thank you, Meb.'

The woman curtseyed and backed toward the door. 'If you need anything during the night, miss, just ring. The pull is there by the bed.' She curtseyed again and left, closing the door behind her.

Nancy saw that her trunks had been brought up to the room and partially unpacked. A nightgown was laid out across the bed for her. The idea of omnipresent servants was going to take some getting used to, Nancy reflected as she undressed. She lay down, wondering how she could possibly sleep after what had happened. How could she sleep in this strange room with Robert lying grievously injured next door? But then the laudanum took hold, her eyes closed of themselves, and she fell into a deep, dreamless sleep.

★　★　★

Nancy Hooker was born and brought up on a fair-sized farm outside of Lexington,

Massachusetts. Her father, Ephraim Benjamin Hooker, was the sort of man the Constitution of the United States was written for: an educated, liberal-minded landholder, willing to accept the responsibility for governing himself. He had served, during his life, both as County Judge and as Alderman, and had consistently resisted pressure to run for higher office. 'I got me a farm to tend to,' Nancy had heard him say more than once to important-looking men who had come down from Boston to speak with him, 'and two growing kids to look after. That's more'n enough work for any man.'

Nancy never knew her mother, who had died of one of those diseases with a vague name that just meant the doctor didn't know what it was or how to help. She and her brother Robert, six years older than Nancy, were brought up by their father with the help of Prudence Walpole, an obscure relative, no longer young, who had come to live with the family after the death of Nancy's mother. Nancy hadn't exactly had an unhappy childhood. She'd been lonelier than average, with her father always busy, her brother away first at boarding school and then at Harvard, and Cousin Prudence speaking so seldom that every statement took on an air of great importance. Prudence Walpole's verbal weapon was the sniff, and she used it constantly. She sniffed disapproval, she sniffed approval, and she sniffed contempt. Her range of sniffs almost exceeded her vocabulary; or so Nancy often thought.

Nancy learned to populate her isolation with imaginary people, and to give a personality to each of the animals on the farm. As she grew up, she found it harder to keep the worlds of reality and imagination separate. She lived mostly in her imagination — until the sudden death of her father jerked her back to reality.

Shortly after Nancy's nineteenth birthday, her father went out one morning in December to hunt for a cow that had strayed during the night. He was found that evening floating face down in the creek where he had broken through the thin ice. It had been a mild winter.

Robert had come home from Harvard

right after the accident, and he stayed to manage the farm. Nancy could guess how much the double shock of losing their father and giving up his studies had hurt her brother, but he never spoke of it. Their life was just starting to settle down to a routine when it was upset again, in a way neither of them could have anticipated.

The man who pulled the trap to a stop in front of the farmhouse and stepped off into the spring mud was dressed in a fashion Nancy had never seen before. The top hat, elaborately conservative suit and vest, and fur-trimmed greatcoat were much more suited to the comforts of a great city than to the rough New England farm. The only concession to weather and climate was the pair of finely tooled boots the gentleman had buckled over the cuffs of his trousers.

'This is the Hooker farm, I believe?' the gentleman asked, taking his top hat off as he addressed Nancy, whom he saw standing in the doorway.

'Yes, sir, it is,' she told him. 'What can I do for you?'

'I would like to speak with Judge Ephraim Benjamin Hooker, if I may.'

Nancy felt her throat muscles tighten, and her head somehow felt isolated from the rest of her body as she fought off a wave of dizziness. The sudden mention of her father's name had brought with it all-too-recent memories of the Judge striding about the farm on the round of never-ending chores. *My father's death was news in every newspaper from here to Boston,* Nancy thought. Who was this stranger with the strange accent who hadn't heard about it?

She found that she was gripping tightly onto the porch railing. 'I'm sorry,' she said, 'but my father died about four months ago.'

'By Jove!' the man cried. 'Look here — I'm terribly sorry. I just arrived from London, and I had no idea. The news must somehow have just missed me as I left. You must be Judge Hooker's daughter, Nancy. Allow me to introduce myself: Sir Andrew Dean. Your father was in communication with me; had he told you about it?'

Nancy shook her head. 'No. Perhaps I'd better get my brother.'

'Ah yes, your brother Robert. Then he is no longer enrolled in that American university — what is it — Harvard?'

'No, sir. Come in and sit down while I fetch him.' Nancy turned and fled from this stranger who knew so much about her family. She found Robert in the barn and told him of the man waiting in their parlor.

'In communication with the Judge, he said,' Robert mused as they crossed the yard to the house. 'There must be letters in the big desk. I've been meaning to go through the papers there, but somehow never got around to it. Well, we'll see what we see.'

Prudence was serving the stranger tea when Nancy and Robert entered the room. With a sniff, she poured for them also and then settled back in a chair out of the way to listen to the proceedings.

'Robert Hooker at your service, sir,' Nancy's brother said, sitting in a straight-backed chair opposite Sir Andrew. Nancy sat on one side of the couch where she could watch the two men.

'Sir Andrew Dean at yours, sir. May I offer my sincere condolences over the death of your father. I rode out here from Boston today fully expecting to find him alive and well. Miss Walpole has told me how the tragedy happened, and I'm extremely sorry to hear the news.'

Nancy looked at Prudence with some mild astonishment. The explanation must have taken more words than Nancy had ever heard Prudence Walpole utter at one time.

'I knew your father only through letters,' Sir Andrew continued, 'but I was looking forward to meeting him. I was favorably impressed by his communications.'

'Letters?' Robert asked.

'You know nothing of our correspondence?'

'No, sir. My father said nothing of it.'

'Well then, perhaps I should start at the beginning. I am a solicitor of the city of London, In this matter I am representing the estate of the late Lord John Hooker, the ninth Baron Benjamin.'

'Baron Benjamin?' Robert asked sharply.

'Yes. A relative of yours. You don't know of him?'

'We didn't discuss the British branch of the family very much.'

'There does seem to be a bit of — er — antipathy in the United States towards Great Britain.'

'We haven't forgotten the Revolutionary War,' Robert said.

'So I note. One would think you hadn't fought in any since then. At any rate, Lord John died without leaving wife, children, or a will. He was in his late twenties and only outlived his father, the eighth Baron Benjamin, by a little over a year. He suffered a broken neck when his horse stumbled on a hunt.'

'What do you hunt from horseback?' Robert asked.

'Foxes,' Sir Robert explained. 'As Oscar Wilde puts it: 'The English country gentleman galloping after a fox — the unspeakable in full pursuit of the uneatable.' We had to trace the family back three generations, to your great-grandfather, to find where the title and the bulk of the estate resides. It's taken us almost two years to firmly establish the right to the title. Your father was the tenth Baron Benjamin; and since his death you have been the eleventh Baron Benjamin.'

'Oh, Bob,' Nancy said, her eyes shining. 'A baron! How exciting.'

'I find in myself what I can only describe as mixed emotions, sir,' Robert told Sir Andrew. 'Suddenly finding myself heir to a title is, as my sister says, heady news. At the same time I can't help feeling that the whole idea is somehow anti-American.'

Sir Andrew made a gesture approaching a shrug. 'I suppose you can refuse to accept. I'm not sure how it's done, but there must be a precedent somewhere in British law. Everything else has happened at one time or another.'

'I guess I'll get used to it,' Robert said, looking at Nancy. 'I don't see how I can turn it down.'

'The title is yours irrevocably,' Sir Andrew said. 'The estate itself is, of course, entailed.'

'In what way, sir?'

'To take possession of the estate you must establish physical residence in Benjamin House, the old baronial manor house. This condition was written into the land patent when it was awarded by Charles the First. Also, besides losing the estate, if you do not take up residence in Benjamin House the title will end with your generation. That is, with you.'

'Isn't that rather unusual?' Robert asked.

'It is extremely unusual. The period of Charles the First produced many oddities in British law. It was, as you know, a very troubled time.'

'What exactly does this estate include?'

'Well, there's the manor house itself: Benjamin House on Benjamin Square. There is enough land and property — including most of the surrounding area, which is now fairly heavily built up — to bring you in an income of some twelve thousand pounds a year.' Sir Andrew smiled and leaned back in his chair. 'You will also inherit a two-hundred-and-fifty-year-old legend.'

'A legend,' Nancy exclaimed. 'Bob,

you're going to be a baron with a legend!'

'Tell me, Sir Andrew, how does one go about inheriting a legend?' Robert asked.

'The legend surrounding Benjamin Square includes a rhyme and a story,' Sir Andrew told them. He reached into an inner pocket. 'I have here a copy of the rhyme; read it and then I'll tell you the story that goes with it.'

Nancy looked over Robert's shoulder as he took the piece of paper, and read it along with him:

'*Face Second Watch from Benjamin*
  Square
Pace out the steps, for you know
  what is there
Left march when you come about
  the great ring
Out, up, to the left, and return to
  the King.'

'Tell me,' Robert asked Sir Andrew, 'does the story that goes with this rhyme tell what it means?'

'That poem, if I may call it that, hides a two-and-a-half-centuries-old secret,' Sir

25

Andrew said. 'That's part of the story. It goes back to the time when King Charles, although still secure on his throne, was first starting to feel the effects of the roundhead armies under Oliver Cromwell and General Monk. In 1643 Sir Thomas Hooker became the first Baron Benjamin; the title was awarded for loyal and exemplary service to his king during the battle of Roundway Down. The estate was created quite close to London, so that Sir Thomas Hooker would always be close to his king.

'As the years passed, Cromwell's armies gained control over more and more territories, and some of Charles's staunchest supporters began to see how the winds of war were blowing. Toward the end, the royalists were few and well separated, and Charles was in hiding, trying to flee the country. One of the places he hid, as a matter of fact — one of the last places he hid in England — was Benjamin House. That was the start of the legend.' Sir Andrew paused to take a sip of tea.

'It sounds like a story out of one of the

romances I used to read,' Nancy said. 'Please, don't stop there.'

'The rest of the story may be fiction. One thing is known for sure: When Charles the First went into hiding, he took his coronet and many of the crown jewels with him. When he surrendered to the Scots, the jewels, some dating back to the reigns of early Plantagenets, were not surrendered with him. Two years later Charles was beheaded, without having revealed the whereabouts of these gems. They disappeared completely, and to this day they haven't been located.

'The legend is that these jewels — the heritage of a nation — were secreted in one of the last places to hide Charles. To be exact, in Benjamin House. According to the story, Sir Thomas Hooker, one of the king's most loyal supporters, was given the mission of guarding the jewels until his safe return. But as you know, the king never returned.'

'Why didn't Lord Benjamin just turn the jewels over to the next king — Charles the Second, wasn't it?' asked Nancy.

'As to that, we can only surmise. Charles the Second landed to claim the crown eleven years after Charles the First lost his head. Thomas Hooker, Lord Benjamin, was an old man by this time. Charles professed to be a Protestant. Perhaps the faithful Thomas was waiting for his Catholic brother, James, to ascend to the crown, and died while still waiting. There are many possibilities.'

'And the poem?' Nancy asked.

'The rhyme is supposed to be a sort of code handed down from baron to baron telling of the location of the treasure. For about the first hundred years, apparently, the poem was kept secret; and by the time it was generally known, the key — if there ever was a key — was missing.'

'The key?' Robert asked.

'The key to the meaning. It sounds like a simple set of directions in rhyme, but when you try to carry them out in any possible way or combination of ways, you find nothing. The treasure guarded by this poem is as elusive as the pot of gold at the end of the rainbow.'

'A fine puzzle,' Robert commented.

'I'm afraid that it is no more than a romantic legend. But you will have plenty of time to experiment and find out for yourself. That is, if you agree to return to London with me and claim your estate.'

'Frankly, sir, I don't see how I can refuse. I'd certainly never be able to live in peace with my sister again if I did.'

'Robert!' Nancy exclaimed. But, as she felt the flush rising to her face, she knew he was right. Here, with all the suddenness that usually meant only bad news, all the dreams of a lonely childhood were about to come true.

★　★　★

'Can we put you up for the night, Sir Andrew?' Robert asked after the new baron had given his London solicitor a huge dinner.

'No, thank you,' Sir Andrew replied. 'I've just enough time to catch the late train back to Boston. My eldest daughter married a Boston lawyer, and has been living on this side of the ocean for longer than I like to think. I'm staying with them, and it's the first time I've seen her since they left London. It will probably be the last, too. I don't really expect to make a habit of crossing the Atlantic in search of missing heirs. I'll be going back to England with you when you leave, so take your time about settling your affairs; I'm in no hurry.'

3

When Nancy woke, it was still dark. She reached over to the side table for the box of wooden matches, but her hand felt only empty air. Then she remembered: the table she was reaching for was over three thousand miles away. In a second she was completely awake and aware of being horribly alone. She sat up in bed and stared out at the darkness. The room seemed to stretch away in all directions, as though it were a giant hall and her bed was in the middle of it.

Here I am, she thought, *in England: lady of a great house, sister to a baron. And I have never been so desperately miserable in my entire life. Would Robert have come here if it weren't for me? If he dies, am I responsible? No, that's silly. He would have come. It's just that I was looking forward to this so much, and now . . . But it's not my fault. It's this place. This awful, old, stone-cold, brooding* house. *It's as if it stood here for three hundred years waiting for Robert to try to enter. It doesn't like Americans. It knows that the last of the true Barons is dead, and it doesn't want interlopers walking the halls.*

I'm being silly, she thought, pulling the comforter up around her shoulders and settling back into the bed. She closed her eyes, but they wouldn't stay closed, and she found herself staring up into the blackness. There wasn't even a speck of light coming in through the window, and Nancy wondered whether the blinds were drawn. She realized that she didn't even know where the window was. She stared around her, trying to find any gradation of light, any hint of grey to relieve the circle of black.

There is a window, she thought. *There must be a window. No one would have a bedroom without a window. Suppose the door were jammed; then there'd be no way to get out. Why would the door be jammed? Why wouldn't there be a window?* She clenched her fists. *I'm behaving like an eight-year-old child, afraid of the dark. I'll just get up and find the window, and see that the door is unjammed. Is there such a word? Well, there is now!*

Nancy slipped out of bed, the hardwood floor sending fingers of cold up her legs. She couldn't remember whether her slippers had been put out or not. She felt around the floor with one foot, but couldn't find them. Arms extended, she gingerly tiptoed across the floor.

The room was big. She went for several steps without encountering anything. Then she was walking on a rug and could put her whole foot down without freezing. There — a bureau in front of her: quite tall, perhaps a highboy. Then, to the left, an armoire. Then blank wall. Back to the right now. Good — here was the mantel. And here, on top of it, a familiar-feeling box. Yes, it was wax vestas. She took one out and struck it, blinding herself in the glow of the little match. After a second her eyes adjusted, and she looked around. There, on the wall to the right, was the window. It was, indeed, covered by thick green velvet curtains.

The match was about to burn her fingers, so she waved it out and went over to the window, drawing the curtains aside. It was a large casement window, the sash made up of many rectangular panes of glass, each the size of Nancy's hand. She sat on the sill for some time, staring out at the familiar sky. The rain had stopped, the clouds had blown away, and the sky was jet-black and pierced with the bright, friendly stars she had spent so many lonely nights staring at in her youth.

Nancy was accustomed to being lonely, but she was not used to being afraid. Now, all at once, she had to handle more fear than she had ever faced before. She was afraid of this country, with its unknown customs and manners. She would not have the foreigner's chance to immerse herself in this new life gradually. She, all at once, had a position, an estate, and a title: it would be sink or swim. She was afraid of the people, her peers, and in some ways even more, the servants she was now mistress of. She was afraid of this house — this damp, cold, stone hulk that had crippled her brother before he could even set foot inside it. She tried telling herself that these vague fears were unreal and silly; that the emotion of fear should be reserved for serious events. But she found that even the thought of facing a tiger did not start the same pounding in her heart as the thought of facing the servants tomorrow, or having tea with some supercilious dowager duchess.

Finally she turned away from the window, allowing the curtains to fall back into place, and raced over to her bed, climbed in and pulled the comforter up to her chin. She felt better now: at least the stars hadn't changed.

It was five or ten minutes later, and Nancy was almost asleep, when she heard the footsteps outside her door. Someone — it sounded like a man — had paused by her door on his way down the long hall. She held her breath and waited for the footsteps to begin again. After a long moment they did; not hurrying away, but striding in a positive manner, like a man on an important errand.

Nancy slowly let out her breath.

Getting out of bed, she went over to the mantel and struck a match, using it to light the candle she found in a holder on the bureau. She felt around in her cloth bag for her travelling clock and pulled it out. It was still running, and the dial showed ten after three. Who could be wandering around the halls at this hour of the morning? Why did he stop at her door? Perhaps it was Doctor Moran — perhaps he had some news about Robert; but, seeing no light under her door, he had decided not to wake her.

Nancy found the robe she had stuffed into the bag. Tying it closely around her, she took up the candle and went quietly out into the hall. The small flame cast an eerie, flickering glow over the sparsely furnished hallway, one that lit a circle ten feet around her and created monstrous shadows before fading to total darkness. The wall was papered in sickly yellow, with great brown blotches that assumed hideous designs. Keeping to the center of the long carpet, Nancy crept forward to Robert's room.

There was no light under the door.

Nancy opened it as silently as she could and tiptoed into the room. Her brother was lying in the center of the four-poster bed, his head swathed in bandages. He was sound asleep, his breathing deep and rhythmic. Nancy gave a great sigh of relief and backed out of the room more quietly than she had entered it.

Then who could have walked by her room? Nancy suddenly remembered the hideous face she had seen at the window the previous afternoon, and a shudder passed through her body. She pictured the man hiding around the next corner, waiting for her to pass. Then she shook her head and smiled. She had always been brought up to judge people by their habits and actions rather than their outward appearance. The poor man, probably one of the servants, who had to go through life with a face like that! Probably a mild and gentle person who loved children and rescued mice from traps.

There was a strange noise coming from somewhere ahead of her, so soft that it was only gradually that she became aware of it: a series of distinct thuds, followed by a pause and then more thudding. Fear and curiosity waged a brief battle within her breast, and curiosity, as it always had, won out. She tiptoed cautiously forward, pausing at each door to see whether the curious sound came from within.

Three doors further on she came to the source of the sound: a door across the hall from the bedrooms that was about a third smaller than the other doors. Nancy decided it must be some sort of closet. But what could be making that thumping sound from within a closet? It was still very muted, even with her ear up against the door. It must be quite soft, or still far away. A room-sized closet? Nancy opened the door.

'Watch it!' someone yelled. Nancy shielded her eyes against the candle flame and took a step forward into the blackness.

There was no floor under her foot. Nancy tried to save herself by grabbing the door frame, but she was too far forward and it wrenched out of her hand as she fell.

4

Light on the periphery of her vision and a blurred . . . *something* before her eyes were the first things Nancy became aware of. She had been unconscious; for how long, she didn't know. She was lying on what felt like a blanket over a hard, cold surface, and a chill was creeping up her spine. Her vision slowly cleared, and the blurred object became a man bending over her.

'Well?' he demanded harshly. 'How do you feel?'

'I . . . I don't know.' Nancy pushed herself to a sitting position. 'What happened? Who are you?' Looking around, she saw that they were in a large room that seemed to be almost bare of furniture. A second man was going slowly around the room, lighting the row of gas fixtures along the walls.

'My name is Alan DeWit,' the man told her, squatting next to her on the floor, 'and you descended on me from that.' He pointed to an open door set in the near wall about twelve feet off the floor.

'I did?'

He nodded. 'Hardly an auspicious way to begin an acquaintance. Are you at all injured?'

'No, I don't seem to be. That's odd — how could I have fallen twelve feet without hurting myself?'

'I caught you. Sprained my arm doing it. Lucky thing I was down here.'

Nancy's first thought was that he was one of the servants; but his perfectly tailored evening dress, with its wide cravat and emerald stick-pin, hardly seemed the garb of a servant. He was also too self-assured and vaguely condescending to occupy that status in life. And *entirely* too self-assured and condescending, Nancy thought, to occupy any status in her life. On principle Nancy did not approve of either quality, and her principles were strongly held.

'What were you doing down here?' Nancy demanded. 'Were you the one making that noise?'

'What noise is that, milady?'

'A — ah, well, sort of plunking sound. I heard it in the hall, and that's what brought me to try that door. Why would anyone build a door that opened onto a twelve-foot drop?'

'It must have served some purpose in former years; but as to what it was, I have no idea. It's supposed to be kept locked. I think that what you heard must have been my game of darts.'

'Darts? But there wasn't any light.'

'I was practicing for blindfold play,' he said, sounding slightly disconcerted for the first time. 'It seemed easier to keep the lights off than to tie a silly rag around my face.'

The story sounded lame to Nancy, but she said nothing, as she had no idea of what else he might have been doing. 'What room is this?' she asked.

'It's known as the Great Hall. These days it's usually used for balls and the like — receptions, that sort of thing.'

'What was it used for in the past?' Nancy asked, looking around. There were sturdy pillars spaced along the walls to support the half-domed ceiling, and the whole was painted a flat white except where moldings and baseboards retained the original oak. The upper part of the walls, above the strange door she had fallen through, was decorated with flags and banners that looked to be centuries old. The floor was parquet, of such fine hard wood that it scarcely showed its age, except for a large area in the center, which was covered with alternating two-foot squares of white and black stone inlaid in an eight-by-eight pattern.

The man who had been lighting the gas jets came up to them now. 'Is that all, sor?' he asked, touching his knuckle to his forehead. With a start that she could scarcely suppress, Nancy recognized the ugly face of the man at the window.

'Miss Nancy — my man, William,' Alan said, seeing her stare. 'Yes, Bill, thank you; that'll be all.'

'Ar'm' William grumped, nodding his head respectfully to Nancy before retreating to sit sullenly on a bench in the corner.

'Now then,' Alan said. 'Horses, mostly;

and chess games.'

'What?' Nancy asked.

'In the past,' Alan explained with condescending patience, 'this hall was used to assemble the household troop, which included cavalry. Those French windows in the back, leading to the garden, were originally large double doors leading to the stables. And that giant chessboard in the middle of the floor was used to play chess, believe it or not, with live pieces. It was considered greatly amusing. The men would hold mock combat over the squares — wins called on points only, no bloodshed — and the loser would be the 'piece' removed from the game. Legend has it that Charles himself played a few games while he was staying here.'

'How do you know so much about this house?' Nancy demanded. 'And what are you doing here at three in the morning?'

Alan looked surprised. 'I assumed you knew,' he said. 'I live here.'

'You do?' The house was more crowded than Nancy thought. Doctor Moran lived there. He had been doctor-in-residence to the eighth Baron Benjamin and had stayed through Lord John Hooker's brief tenure. He was completing some important biological experiments in a small but complete laboratory set up in an unused coach house in the rear. Or so he and Sir Andrew had informed her. And now Nancy had discovered a second tenant in Benjamin House. She wondered how many more surprises the house held for her.

Alan nodded. 'I had a slight disagreement with my family, and was forced to change my residence. Lord Benjamin — the last Lord Benjamin — was an old schoolmate of mine, and he was kind enough to offer me digs here. If you'd prefer that I move, of course . . . ' He let the rest of the sentence hang.

'That will be up to my brother,' Nancy said. 'When he — if he . . . '

'Naturally,' Alan said, stepping into the gap of her uncompleted thought. 'We'll speak of it another time. Right now, perhaps we should all get some sleep.' He picked up the candle she had dropped in her sudden entrance to the ballroom and relit it for her. 'Shall I escort you to your room?'

'Where is your room?' Nancy asked.

'In the other wing, around that way.' Alan pointed. 'Down at the end of the hall.'

'I see,' Nancy took the candle. 'Thank you for your offer, but I think I can find the way back to my room by myself. I'll be more careful going through doorways.'

He smiled. 'Thank you for dropping in.'

Nancy went back to her room by way of the main staircase, carefully closing the small door when she came to it. She could see Alan and his man William quenching the gaslights in the ballroom below when she closed the door. *Darts,* she thought skeptically as she settled into bed. *I wonder if he really was playing darts in the dark down there. It would explain the sound, but it's such a strange thing to be doing. And, since he lives in the other wing of the house, who was it I heard pass by my room?* She fell asleep with the day's questions and problems whirling about in her brain, and she dreamed of tiptoeing dartboards and falling stones.

5

In a back room of the house on Benjamin Square, two men were still awake. 'It's working well,' one of them said. 'We can begin again tomorrow night.'

The second one looked up from the documents he was studying. 'What of the new Baron Benjamin?'

'Harmless. The stone didn't kill him, but it did the next best thing. He won't be about to bother us for some time.'

'And the woman?'

'The woman? Just that — a homesick, frightened young woman. She won't bother us either. She'd better not. It's been too long and we're too close now to allow her to get in our way.'

The second man folded the papers he had been studying and thrust them back into a large manila folder. 'Right, then. Tomorrow night it is.' They shook hands and the first man smiled.

6

Despite her late hours, Nancy awoke early. She washed herself at the basin and then opened one of the two large trunks and removed a simple green cotton frock that she thought would be suitable for the morning. 'It had better be,' she told herself. 'I have precious little else.' She wondered what the servants would think of her when they unpacked the trunks and discovered that most of one trunk was linens, blankets and towels and the like.

How easily, Nancy reflected, one became accustomed to the idea of proper servants. Cousin Prudence and the hired woman and she had slaved over those two trunks to get everything in. The image of Prudence came into her mind, and Nancy realized how much she missed her sturdy, no-nonsense companion. Prudence Walpole had gone to Philadelphia to visit a sister no one remembered she had. She would be along to join them in England presently; there had somehow been no question from either side about their leaving her behind. Prudence had aided the Hookers in their misfortunes, and she would share fully in the Hooker fortune. The first word of her coming would probably be her arrival, as Nancy doubted that Prudence would cable the date of her leaving. It would never occur to a self-sufficient woman like Prudence Walpole to require anyone to meet her at the dock when she was perfectly capable of hiring a four-wheeler by herself, thank you.

Staring into the mirror on the vanity, Nancy adjusted the frock on her thin frame, carefully combed her hair, and left the room. Her first stop was her brother's room, where she found Doctor Moran already in attendance.

'Good morning, Doctor,' she said. 'How is he?'

'Your brother seems to be doing well,' Doctor Moran replied. 'It's hard to tell for certain until he regains consciousness, but his life signs are strong, and that happy moment could come at any time now. Any signs of serious concussion would surely have shown up by now.'

Nancy walked over to the side of the bed and took Robert's hand. His face was still extremely pale, but his breathing was normal and unlabored. Nancy tried to find reassurance in the doctor's words, but the yards of bandage swathed around Robert's head were not reassuring. 'His hand feels so cold,' she said, 'so very cold. Are you sure he'll be all right? Isn't there anything else we can do?'

'In cases like this, nature does the healing. We doctors can but sit by and give what aid we know how. But from all the signs I can discern, Lord Benjamin's coma should lapse within a day or so, and then he'll be well on the way to recovery.'

Nancy fancied that she heard doubt in Doctor Moran's voice; doubt that he clearly was not going to tell her about. She could only wish, as she went down to breakfast with her brother's bandaged face still in her imagination, that she knew whether the doctor were being truthful or professionally reassuring. If honest, the issue was still in doubt; if dishonest, then she had no way of judging how bad Robert's injuries really were.

She was alone at breakfast. Doctor Moran had already eaten; and Alan DeWit, she learned, never dined with the family. 'Indeed, miss,' the maid told her, 'he's seldom here at all.'

After breakfast, a sepulchral man attired in formal black presented himself to her. 'I am Fenton,' he told her in an impassive nasal voice. 'I have had the honor of being butler to the late Baron Benjamin and, for some thirty-five years, to his father, Sir Paul Hooker. In my youth I was in livery in the household of Admiral Charles Hooker, the seventh Baron Benjamin.' He said no more, but continued standing at respectful attention, his gaze focused somewhere over Nancy's left ear.

Stern and disapproving, Nancy thought. *Fenton is not prepared to like the American branch of the family. And how does one comport oneself when one is faced with one's butler for the first time?* 'Very good, Fenton,' she said, trying to meet his gaze, which stubbornly remained fixed over her head. She was tempted to stand up and see whether he shifted his gaze to the ceiling, but decided that would be childish. 'I am sure you will give my brother, Lord Benjamin, and me the same loyal service you have shown our family through these many years.'

'Indeed,' Fenton said emotionlessly. 'It will, of course, be my privilege to continue serving his lordship and yourself.'

That's settled, Nancy told herself. *I was afraid for a moment that he was about to give notice.*

Fenton continued to stare over Nancy's ear for another minute, then his gaze shifted to the toast-rack. 'Ahem,' he said.

'Yes, Fenton?'

'With Miss Nancy's permission, the servants are assembled in the front hall to meet Miss Nancy. The, ah, ceremony was to take place yesterday evening; but due to the unfortunate, ah, circumstance of Lord Benjamin's, ah, unfortunate accident, it — the ceremony — was put off until this morning. If Miss Nancy doesn't mind.'

Stern and disapproving? Nancy wondered. Or trying not to show the human concern and sympathy about the 'unfortunate accident' that it was clearly not his place to show? Or merely trained out of showing any sort of emotion by his many years of service? Only time would tell. 'Of course, Fenton,' she said. 'I'll be out in a minute.'

'Very good, Miss Nancy.' And, with a stiff bow, he left the breakfast room.

She took a deep breath and squared her shoulders. Now she must face a lineup of British servants who were certainly as snobbish in their way as the upper class were in theirs. This, her shaking knees told her, would be as much of an ordeal as that first tea with a lady she was so frightened of. If in any way she herself were not a proper lady, 'Miss Nancy' or no, she would lose the respect of her own household.

But there was no way around it. So, with horrible images of what might happen, she rose to her feet, straightened her frock, took hold of her trembling nerves, and walked calmly to the door.

The servants were lined up in a row when she entered the hall. The women's uniforms were starched and neat, and the men's livery was spotless and smart, brass buttons shining. Nancy was very conscious of her own worn, travel-rumpled green cotton. She lifted her head a little higher and went to meet them.

'Mrs. Toby, the housekeeper,' Fenton introduced. She curtseyed low, her stiff black dress sweeping the floor in front of her. Her large keyring was worn like a badge of office on her belt.

'Miss Nancy,' she said.

'Cook,' Fenton said, continuing down the line. The little plump woman smiled and bobbed up and down, her large white apron flapping in front of her like a sail. Nancy wondered whether the woman had a name, or did her friends call her 'Cook' on her day off?

'Meb,' Fenton said.

'We've met,' Nancy said. 'Good morning, Meb.'

'Morning, Miss Nancy,' Meb said cheerfully, to the accompaniment of a well-practiced, excellent curtsey.

Fenton indicated the last three women: two healthy, solid lasses in their early twenties, and a short, skinny, pale-faced youngster of no more than fourteen who was trying hard to keep her eyes straight ahead but kept darting frightened glances at Nancy. 'Alice, Jane: housemaids. Little Dwiggens, the scullion.'

Little Dwiggens, Nancy reflected, *looks as frightened as I am.*

'Piggins, the steward,' Fenton intoned.

Piggins bowed stiffly, and Nancy recognized him as the man who had opened the door for them the day before. His little turned-up mustache gave him a bristly, military look. 'Miss,' he said.

'Piggins,' she replied.

'Mr. Burke and Mr. Pitt,' Fenton said, 'the grooms.'

They looked, Nancy decided, like characters from Alice in Wonderland: Mr. Pitt was Tweedledum, and Mr. Burke — Mr. Burke was the rabbit! Tweedledum and the White Rabbit, dressed in top hats and red velvet jackets, with black breeches and ancient, heavily polished black boots. Tweedledum was slightly bow-legged, and the rabbit had soft, fuzzy whiskers and a red nose.

'Marning, merss,' Tweedledum said, doffing his top hat and holding it gingerly over his stomach.

'Welcome,' the White Rabbit said, nodding his head rapidly up and down, with his hat held like a rifle in one arm.

'Mr. Pitt is acting as coachman, as Boswell is ill,' Fenton explained.

'Oh, I'm sorry,' Nancy said. 'I hope it's nothing serious.'

'He has a slight, ah, functional disorder which requires him to spend much of his time flat on his, ah, front. He is being cared for by a sister in Shoreditch. We expect him back with us in a few weeks.'

'That's good,' Nancy said, turning around. The line of servants was staring at her curiously. She realized that they expected her to say something. For a minute her mind went blank; she could think of nothing at all to say. She cleared her throat while the servants waited expectantly. 'I'm glad to meet you all,' she said desperately. 'I'm sure I shall get to know each of you better in a short while.

You must be excellent at your jobs or you wouldn't be here. There will be no changes made in your routine for the time being. I shall discuss that with Fenton and Mrs. Toby in the near future. That will be all for now; thank you all.'

Mrs. Toby stepped forward and slapped her hands together in one sharp clap. 'All right, now. Back to work, all of you!' And in short seconds the hall was clear, except for Nancy and Fenton.

'When do you want to see about engaging the remainder of the staff?' Fenton asked.

'The remainder of the staff?'

'Yes, Miss Nancy. This, of course, is only a skeleton staff, so to speak. Some of the old staff were retired under the old baron's will. And, of course, we haven't replaced any who left since the young baron's death. This is only about a third of the staff required to keep the house open.'

'I see,' Nancy said. 'I assume you and Mrs. Toby are competent to see to the hiring?'

'Yes, miss.'

'Then do. But take your time; I'm afraid it will be a while before we do any entertaining in this house.'

'Very well, Miss Nancy.'

If, indeed, there would ever again be entertaining, or any cause for laughter in this house. Fenton left the room, and Nancy's spirits, artificially buoyed by the need to deal with the servants, dropped to the soles of her feet. She felt so small in this great house. Mistress of Benjamin House, although its lord lay unconscious in an upstairs bedroom. Mistress of this house in which she felt less at home than any of the servants. Mistress of a house with a great and frightening history. The very room she was in, a reception room, was hung with the portraits of great lords and ladies — she assumed they were early Benjamins — staring at her. Frozen in their frames, they looked down at Nancy through the remove of centuries, and they saw her, and they did not approve.

A bell rang in the back of the house, and a few seconds later Nancy heard the tread of footsteps to the front door.

'Ah, good morning, Fenton.' It was Sir

Andrew's voice. 'Tell me, how is Lord Robert today?'

'Unchanged, so says Doctor Moran,' Fenton replied. 'He is expected to regain consciousness within the next twenty-four hours.'

Nancy was glad to note that the doctor gave a consistent story to others. Perhaps it was true.

'That is good news. Is Miss Nancy at home?'

'I'll see, sir.'

'Tell her I've brought guests.'

Nancy was tempted to hide, but there was nowhere to go. She went bravely into the hall. 'Sir Andrew, how good to see you.'

'Ah, Miss Nancy!' He came over to her and clasped her hand between his. 'I hope you won't think it outrageous of me — I've brought over two of your neighbors to meet you.' He indicated the two women standing just inside the great door. One was old, with a face like a curious raven and sparkling eyes; the other was scarcely as old as Nancy herself, a delicate-featured woman whose face would look plain if frozen on a canvas but had a sensitive, vibrant beauty in life.

Sir Andrew gave a courtly half-bow, looking very pleased with himself. 'Allow me to present the Duchess of Llewelyn and her granddaughter, Lady Gayle. Your grace, may I present Miss Nancy Hooker, sister of Robert Hooker, Baron Benjamin.'

The duchess passed Sir Andrew like a man of war passing a schooner and took Nancy's hand. 'Dowager Duchess,' she said. 'Call me Aunt Gwen. For the past thirty years everybody has called me that — everybody who will speak to me at all. It's such a pleasure to meet you, my dear. Sir Andrew has told me of your trying experiences. You must tell me all about America. Have you ever met any Indians? I knew an Indian at one time, but he was a maharajah. A delightful man. Gave me an elephant. Couldn't think what to do with an elephant. Ended up giving it to the Leeds Zoological Gardens. My dear, you have no idea how much an elephant eats. Let me introduce my granddaughter,

Lady Gayle. Gayle, come over here! You two should get along fine; you have very little in common. That will give you a lot to talk about.'

Lady Gayle extended a gloved hand to Nancy. 'We are so curious about life in America,' she said. 'You must tell us all about it.'

Nancy took the hand, trying to decide whether Lady Gayle was being interested or patronizing. She couldn't help contrasting the beautiful green satin suit Lady Gayle was wearing with her own worn frock. 'I would be pleased to tell you about life in America,' she said, leading the way to the front sitting-room, 'if you would reciprocate by telling me about London society. It's quite a big jump, crossing the Atlantic Ocean, and I do feel out of place and unsure of myself.'

'Nonsense!' Duchess Llewelyn declared, sitting herself firmly on the center of the sofa, with her skirts spread around her like the foothills of a formidable mountain. 'You're a personable, intelligent young woman; you will do well here. Hundreds of beaux in no time.'

'Grandmama is quite outspoken,' Lady Gayle said.

'Grandmama has been quite outspoken for the past thirty years,' Sir Andrew said, perching himself in a straight-backed chair.

'Thank you, Andrew, for stopping at thirty,' Duchess Llewelyn said. 'Miss Hooker, I welcome you to London.'

'Thank you,' Nancy said. 'But if I'm to call you Aunt Gwen, then you must call me Nancy.'

'I was well acquainted with the old Baron Benjamin,' Duchess Llewelyn went on. 'Your grand-uncle however many times removed. Lady Benjamin and I were great friends. She died young of what the doctors called a blood disorder, a term greatly in fashion in those days to describe medical ignorance. You don't look a bit like her; don't remind me of her at all. Do you believe in reincarnation?'

'Excuse me?' Nancy asked.

'She would have come back as a sleek, furred animal. Perhaps an otter, or one of those foxes gentlemen take such delight in chasing all over the countryside. No matter. Is there anything you need, anything we can do to make you more comfortable in our great city?'

'I haven't thought — ' Nancy began.

'Of course not. You should see something of London. Do some shopping. Get out of this great mass of stone. A shopping expedition is what you need. Someone to show you around. Gayle, what are you doing this afternoon?'

'Really,' Nancy said, 'I couldn't — '

'Nonsense! Of course you could.'

'A shopping expedition is just what I had in mind, Grandmama,' Lady Gayle said. 'I would be delighted if you would come with me, Nancy.'

'But,' Nancy said, 'I shouldn't leave . . . the house.'

'Your brother is in good hands,' Sir Andrew said, guessing what Nancy was worrying about, 'and it will do you good to get out.'

'Sir Andrew is taking me to see a thingummy — a telephone. Says I should have one in my house. His last enthusiasm was for a steam-carriage that cut great blessed ruts in my macadam drive before expiring noisily on the east lawn in the midst of the annual charity tea. I want to investigate this telephone before Andrew has one installed. Make sure it doesn't emit some subtle vibration that will shake down the house. One is supposed to be able to speak over great distances to anyone else who possesses a telephone. I am not convinced that this is an advantage. Have you ever seen a telephone?'

'Yes,' Nancy replied. 'They have them in Boston.'

'I'm sure they do,' Duchess Llewelyn said. 'You and Gayle will spend the day shopping. Get to know each other.'

Nancy was too overawed to argue with the older woman, and she was forced to admit to herself that getting out of the house for a few hours was a good idea. She excused herself to go upstairs and change into a traveling costume. When she reached her room, she discovered that since she had gone down to breakfast, all her trunks had been unpacked and the clothing and other belongings put neatly away.

The white percale shirtwaist she wanted was neatly folded in the middle drawer of her dresser. She put it on the bed and found the newest suit she had hanging in the closet. She had bought it from the Montgomery Ward catalogue only three months before, and had never expected to wear it in London. An occasional trip to Boston — and this suit was quite elegant enough for that.

5700 Ladies' Newport Suit, ready-made, consists of jacket and skirt to be worn with shirt waists. Jacket is made with tuxedo back, large leg-o'-mutton sleeves, wide revers in front, double stitched seams, inside seams bound, new organ-piped skirt, very full and wide, deep turned hem at bottom. Made of good-looking and serviceable repellent cloth, in navy blue or black.

Nancy's was navy blue. Serviceable repellent cloth. As Nancy put it on, it felt like canvas sacking to her fingers; cheap, dull, stiff, heavy, and altogether unfashionable and undesirable. *This,* she told herself as she worked the buttons of the jacket through the stiff buttonholes, *is silly. The suit is quite nice and suitable for London weather. The material is fine. It isn't cut or stitched as well as Lady Gayle's, but it will do. It will have to do!* Nancy spent some time in front of the mirror, arranging her hair, and then left the room.

As she opened her door, she heard footsteps receding down the hall, and a dark figure turned the corner to the service stairway. Had someone been listening outside her door? Listening for what? She ran down the hall, but when she reached the stairs they were empty. Nancy climbed the narrow staircase to the next floor. The upstairs hallway was also deserted. It ran off into a warren of rooms and corridors leading to storage areas and servants' quarters.

Nancy went silently down the hall, listening for retreating footsteps, but there was no sound but the rustle of her own skirt. The casement window at the end of the hall was open, and she paused to look out. The day was fresh and clear, with no trace of fog. The trees and rooftops in the distance looked as if they had been etched with a fine-line stylus and colored with pure unmixed oils. It was a beautiful and magical view of her new city of London.

The driveway arched beneath her, with the wide steps leading to the front door to her right. Nancy suddenly realized that this must be where Alan DeWit's man, William, watched them arrive. A foot-wide ledge that ran the width of the building passed right below the window. Nancy noticed what looked like a gap in the ledge to her right. Curious, she tried the handle of the door to the right. It opened easily, revealing a small room with a row of gun racks around the walls. The racks were filled with identical muskets of an ancient pattern. Sealed wooden boxes with rope handles were stacked carefully in the center of the room. Nancy was somewhat familiar with guns, as might be expected of a gentleman farmer's daughter, and she paused to examine the ones racked along the wall.

Most of them were rusted, and looked long unused, although a little work could probably put them in order again; but the four next to the door were polished and shiny, showing recent care. *Someone's been using these*, she thought, *and quite recently. How curious.* She would remember to inquire about it; probably Fenton would be the one to ask.

She went over to the window and opened it, finding another anomaly: even though the room was thick with dust, and looked as if it hasn't been cleaned in the past fifty years, the window lock and hinges were newly oiled and the window swung open freely and easily.

The hole in the ledge was right below this window: a square gap where the top stone was missing from the two-layer shelf. *That must be it*, Nancy thought. *That's where the stone that hit Robert sat for two hundred years. We thought it came from the overhang on the roof but it must have dislodged from here.* Nancy leaned out to get a better look at the gap, and found that her heart was throbbing in her chest.

There was a row of fine grooves in the stone below the gap! The space was at least a foot wide. The missing stone had rested firmly in place, supported by the one below. There was no way it could have fallen. Someone must have pushed it off the ledge!

Someone tried to kill Robert. Someone, in this land of strangers, hated my brother enough to drop a huge stone on him. Why? Why would anyone . . . We didn't even know any of the people here. Who . . . ?

Alan!

Alan DeWit. It must be. His man was at the next window, probably to tell him when we were directly below. But he missed. Will he try again? I don't even know why he tried once. What can I do?

The police? What could she tell them? A stone fell next to her brother, and the ledge looked too wide for the stone to have dropped by itself, so she suspected that a man who had never met her brother was trying to murder him? The police wouldn't believe that; and if they did, there wouldn't be anything they could do about it. She'd be lucky if they didn't think her insane.

There was only one thing to do. She would have to find out for herself why Alan DeWit was trying to murder her brother. He must have a motive, and she should be able to find it out.

Would he try again? Was it enough to have Robert incapacitated, or was it necessary for whatever scheme Alan was following to have him dead? She would have to find some way to guard Robert from any more 'accidents'.

Nancy closed the window and left the room, slowly walking downstairs while she decided what she must do. How would the next attack come? Something in his food? When Robert awoke from his coma, she would prepare his meals. Someone entering his room in the dead of night? She couldn't stay awake all night to watch. There must be some way. Perhaps she could hire a night nurse. Doctor Moran would probably say that Robert didn't need one, but Nancy could insist that she was worried. She wouldn't have to specify what she was worried about. They might think she was being silly, but that wouldn't matter.

Suppose — Nancy stopped and put her fist to her mouth — *Suppose it isn't just Robert he's after? He might want to kill me too. How can I guard Robert and myself at the same time? What does he want? Why is he doing this?* She had the feeling that she had fallen into a nightmare and didn't know how to wake up. Could it be that she was imagining all this? Could the stone have fallen in some perfectly innocent manner? She tried to imagine an innocent manner in which a twenty-pound stone could have pushed itself over a foot of ledge and then off. She shook her head and continued downstairs. This would have to be thought out, and she must be careful. If there were only someone she could confide in in this great, ancient stone mansion. If only, in all of England, there were someone she could trust. She had never felt so alone in all of her lonely childhood, or so frightened.

But there wouldn't be any time for fear if she were to do everything she had to. It seemed that the price of having all her childhood dreams come true was a sudden end to childhood.

7

Lady Gayle and Nancy rode into London in the Benjamin coach. Nancy had never felt so grand in her life as she sat in her own private carriage with the Benjamin arms embossed on the doors. She promised herself that she would enjoy this first trip into London; that she would put aside her troubles for the excitement of a visit to the city of Dickens and Thackeray.

'The first thing we must do,' Lady Gayle informed her, 'is get you some gloves.'

'Gloves?' Nancy said. 'I had a pair . . . I must have mislaid . . . '

'One does not go out, particularly in public places, without a pair of gloves. One doesn't have to wear them, you understand; merely holding them and swishing them about as one speaks is quite sufficient. But one must have the gloves. The rules of etiquette are quite strict on that point. Is anything wrong,

Nancy? You seem quite distracted. Is there anything I can do? Would you like some smelling-salts?'

'No,' Nancy assured her. 'Thank you. I'm quite all right.'

'We are passing Madame Tussaud and Sons' Waxworks Museum, there on our left. I shall take you for a visit; the new Chamber of Horrors is quite thrilling. Perhaps it will cheer you up.'

'Not right now, thank you,' Nancy said.

'Right. Onward to the gloves.'

'Tell me something about Alan DeWit,' Nancy said suddenly. She felt as if she'd blurted it out, but aside from a sharp glance that might have signified most anything, Lady Gayle didn't seem to have noticed anything unusual.

'Alan DeWit,' Lady Gayle mused. 'He is something of a mystery, you know.'

'No,' Nancy declared, 'I didn't know.'

'The last baron's houseguest. He is still in residence at Benjamin House, I take it?'

Nancy nodded.

'He's Lord Alan, you know.'

'No,' Nancy said, 'I didn't.'

'Yes. He'd be some sort of remote relative of yours. Son of old Lord Paul's wife's sister, so he was first cousin to Lord John. The sister married well: his father is the Earl of DeWit. Name and title. DeWit of DeWit, you know. Alan is a younger son. He's been unofficially disowned by the earl. Kicked out a few years ago — right before he came to live a Benjamin house.'

'Why?' Nancy asked.

'That's not clear. All sorts of gossip. It's said he's a gambler. It's also said that that's not his only vice. Grandmama says one should believe only ten percent of what one sees, and nothing of what one hears. I must say that the stories about Alan DeWit give one a lot to disbelieve.'

'I see,' Nancy said. 'That's . . . fascinating. What sort of stories?'

'Well, he has been seen at all hours in all sorts of places. Of course, one always wonders what the people who report such things were doing in these places themselves. But one is always too polite to ask. And he does all sorts of things, or so one is told. That's not too specific, is it?'

'No,' Nancy admitted,' it isn't.'

'Well, gambling halls, for one thing. It is said that Alan inherited over twenty thousand pounds on his twenty-first birthday, and had gambled it away — lost it all — within three or four months. He frequents a private club called The Blades; been going there since it opened. After he lost the money, he had a violent fight with his father and moved out. That's when he came to live with John.'

'So he's broke,' Nancy said.

'Broke?'

'That means he doesn't have any money.'

'Ah. Broke. That's an interesting point. Alan DeWit seems to have sufficient money for his needs — and his needs are quite extravagant. As I said, he still goes to that Blades establishment. I would imagine that takes money. Although where he gets it from, I have no idea. That is part of the mystery. Then there are the women . . . ' Lady Gayle paused for effect.

'Women?'

Lady Gayle smiled and twirled a glove.

'Actresses, dance-hall women; that sort. He escorts these, ah, women to some of the best places in the city. Seems to enjoy shocking people. Sometimes it seems he actually goes out of his way to create an effect. And, I can assure you, he succeeds.'

This gave Nancy a lot to think about. Throughout the visit to the glove shop and the mercer's she tried to get more information from Gayle, who was firm in insisting that she drop the 'Lady'. But, although Gayle was more than willing to gossip about Alan DeWit, she had no more information. And the picture she drew of Alan was more that of a spoiled child than an evil man. It made Alan seem even a bit glamorous and adventurous. Not that Nancy thought gambling to be a good thing, but somehow she didn't think it engendered the sort of evil represented by murder. Nancy admitted to herself that her only knowledge of gambling was through the sort of novels her father and brother called 'trash' and couldn't understand her reading.

Gayle introduced Nancy to Madame

Fortuno, her dressmaker, who had her shop in the Strand above a gentleman who advertised himself as a 'Porpoise Hide Boot Maker'. This was when Nancy learned about the British 'first floor', which was where Americans placed their second floor: one flight above the British 'ground floor'.

Madame Fortuno was an old woman with a ramrod-straight back and grey hair in a severely tidy bun. She was garbed in a well-tailored black suit and had a mouthful of pins. Her brown eyes sparkled through her rimless glasses, and she danced when she walked. She examined the fabric they brought up to her, and then closely examined Nancy, walking slowly around her several times, making continuous 'umm' and 'ahh' sounds, and occasionally skipping for one or two steps.

'The figure!' she said. 'The posture!' She made a circular motion with her finger. 'Walk around the room.'

Nancy walked around the room.

'The walk!' Madame Fortuno said. Then she attacked Nancy with a tape measure, clapping her hands together and jotting down numbers on a small card. 'I make up dummy of you,' she said. 'Then make dresses, skirts, jackets; whatever you say. Very good: good figure, good posture, good walk. Very good. You leave everything to me.'

'I'll leave everything to you,' Nancy agreed, slightly overawed by all this attention. She took Gayle's advice as to what she would need and left an order for three tea gowns, two morning frocks, and assorted shirtwaists and wrappers. It wasn't until they had left Madame Fortuno's that she realized that at no time had there been any discussion of the cost of all this.

'Tell me,' she asked Gayle, 'does a lady not concern herself with the price of things?'

'A lady,' Gayle told her, 'haggles over every farthing. In a ladylike fashion, you understand. Madame Fortuno can be trusted to keep her fees reasonable.'

'It's just that I have no idea of what things should cost over here,' Nancy said.

'We shall conspire together until you

are better acquainted with our money and our prices.'

They stopped to lunch at the ladies' grill of the Northumberland Hotel, and Nancy spent the time telling Gayle of life in Massachusetts. Gayle seemed sincerely interested, and listened closely. At first Nancy was hesitant, thinking Gayle was being polite or patronizing; but when she saw that the interest was unfeigned, she found herself talking more and more freely. She spoke of the woods in autumn, and of pumpkins, and of walking through frost-covered fields staked by occasional dead cornstalks. She told Gayle of summers spent paddling her birch canoe, and of her special place on a small island in the middle of Lake Kannehautuck. She talked about picnics and parades and Fourth of July celebrations, when the whole sky was alight all night with streaks and bursts of color. But mostly, she found, she talked about herself.

'It sounds like it must have been very lonely,' Gayle said after a pause.

'I didn't mean it to sound that way,' Nancy said, afraid that self-pity had crept in to her storytelling.

'Perhaps not,' Gayle said, smiling, 'but I am very good at recognizing loneliness. People with a common affliction can often see the symptoms in each other when they would be unrecognized by the outside observer.'

'I would have never have thought of you,' Nancy said. 'I mean, your father's a duke, and . . . and . . . ' She stopped in confusion.

'Oh, yes,' Gayle said, 'Daddy. He lives most of the time in India, you know. Empire and all that. Mother spent a few years out, but couldn't stand it. She came back to live in London. I spent my childhood in a very exclusive school for young ladies, and at Bratteltum.'

'Bratteltum?'

'Our estate. It's quite large. I shall take you to visit; you'll like it. You can teach me to build a canoe. We have our own lake.'

Nancy took Gayle's hand. 'We must do that.'

'Grandmama would be very disappointed with your stories,' Gayle said.

'You should find a way to insert an Indian somewhere.'

'I'll reread my *Deerslayer*,' Nancy promised, laughing. 'We must do nothing to disappoint your grandmother.'

They decided, at Gayle's insistence, that they would visit Madame Tussaud and Sons' Waxworks Museum on the way home. Nancy didn't want to stay away too long, but a half-hour stop at the museum might be pleasant.

They left the restaurant and called for the carriage. In a few moments it arrived, with Mr. Pitt in the driver's seat like Tweedledum perched on the wall. 'Very curious coincidence,' Gayle said as they settled back for the ride.

'What sort of very curious coincidence?' Nancy asked.

'The hansom that pulled up behind us was the same one that was behind us when we stopped at Madame Fortuno's. There must be five thousand cabs in the city; think of the slight chance of the same one being behind us twice. Picture separate lives almost intertwining twice, like part of some grand pattern. Perhaps it's some darkly handsome young man, and we are fated to meet.'

'More likely two different passengers,' Nancy said.

'Does so little romance flutter beneath your breast?'

'How do you know it's the same cab? They all look alike.'

'But horses,' Gayle said, 'are more individual than people. The same man could pass me ten times a day, and I might not notice, unless he were particularly handsome or striking. People are all so dreadfully the same. But horses differ in size, shape, color, markings, breadth, ear shape, nose, mane, temperament, teeth, and a thousand other things.'

'This horse was different?' Nancy asked, intrigued.

'This horse,' Gayle assured her, 'was unique.'

'Describe for me this unique horse.'

Gayle leaned back and closed her eyes. 'Yellow,' she said. 'Not tan, mind you, but yellow. Swaybacked, poor thing. Mottled. Altogether an unhealthy-looking horse. With a black stocking on its right foreleg, and a black mask over both eyes, like some sort of equine bandit. A memorable animal.'

'Unique,' Nancy agreed. 'Perhaps it's this horse that's due to enter your life. Or the driver. What did the driver look like?'

'The jarvey?' Gayle shrugged. 'I really didn't notice. When you've seen one mud-stained top hat, you've seen every mud-stained top hat.'

They alighted in front of Madame Tussaud's large building on Marylebone Road. 'That's very impressive,' Nancy said, staring up at the four-story brick structure.

'It wasn't always this grand,' Gayle said. 'The old place in Baker Street was much less assuming.'

'Baker Street!' Nancy said. 'You mean there *is* a Baker Street?'

'Certainly. My old dressmaker is there, the one I used before I met Madame Fortuno. Why shouldn't there be a Baker Street?'

'There should,' Nancy explained. 'But I didn't know there was. That's where Sherlock Holmes lives.'

'Oh!' Gayle laughed. 'The consulting detective. I didn't know those stories were popular across the ocean.'

'They are with me! I read every one that comes out. I was brokenhearted when I discovered that Sherlock Holmes and Doctor Watson were fictional characters.'

'Let's go inside,' Gayle said suddenly, and hurried up to the ticket booth.

'Just step inside, misses,' the uniformed porter said. Then Nancy realized that the woman in the outside ticket booth, who had been carefully ignoring them, was a wax figure. The real booth was right inside the door, and Gayle purchased two tickets and they went on in.

'Why the hurry?' Nancy asked as Gayle rushed them inside.

'That is stretching coincidence too far,' Gayle said.

'Gayle, what are you talking about?' Nancy asked.

'My father has a saying: 'Once is happenstance, twice is coincidence, three times is enemy action.''

'Gayle!'

'Perhaps we should find a consulting detective.'

'Would you please tell me?' Nancy asked.

'A hansom cab pulled up while we were standing outside.'

'Yes?'

'It was pulled by the most interesting horse. I would call it unique. I *have* called it unique.'

'Oh,' Nancy said. 'That is strange. Did you see who was in it?'

'No, I didn't wait. Perhaps if we stand here, he'll come in after us. Or perhaps he'll just wait outside and abduct us as we leave.'

'Abduct us!' Nancy shivered. 'Gayle, you have a morbid mind. Nobody wants to abduct us.'

'I've read of such things, here in the city. Women are disappearing all the time, only to turn up years later dancing in some show in Germany or in the harem of some fat sheik.'

'Now listen,' Nancy said. 'Look at these people coming in. Which of them do you think is going to abduct us?' A husband and wife were entering the museum, she short and dowdy but pleasant-looking, he very thin and straight, with a bowler that just reached the bridge of his nose. Behind them was a party of schoolgirls chattering and giggling their way down the hall.

'Then he's waiting outside,' Gayle insisted.

'Nonsense,' Nancy said firmly. 'Besides, he wouldn't dare do anything with all these people around. We'll just go outside and confront him.'

'Nancy!' Gayle said, allowing herself to be pulled toward the door. 'Are you sure you weren't raised by Indians?'

'We'll be right back,' Nancy called to the ticket-taker as they hurried by.

The street outside was devoid of hansom cabs. A growler pulled up by the curb, discharging two adults and a melee of small children. There were no loungers in sight, suspicious or otherwise. The Benjamin carriage was not in evidence, as Nancy had given Pitt permission to take half an hour and have a cup of tea.

'There,' Nancy said, spreading her

hand to indicate the whole street. 'Are you satisfied?'

Gayle sighed. 'Whenever the practical meets the romantic, I suppose it is the romantic that must give in.'

'You think it's romantic to be kidnapped by a gang of ruffians and carried off to wherever?'

'Not when it happens,' Gayle admitted. 'But think of the stories you could tell afterward!'

'I have a feeling that most of the stories couldn't be told in polite company.'

They went back inside. The museum's rooms were large and airy, each being organized around one particular topic or theme. Political figures graced one room, each amazingly lifelike, and with an air of naturalness that made it seem that any second they would come to life and continue with whatever they were doing. President Lincoln, top hat in hand, was leaning his tall body over to speak with a child, while Disraeli continued an angry speech to a nonexistent crowd. Queen Victoria was frozen in the act of imperially descending from the royal coach.

Another room had detailed historical scenes. There Nelson stood on the top deck of the *Victory* as it cut through the French fleet at Trafalgar. Gayle stopped to admire a scene of Cromwell arguing with Charles the First. 'I'd like to hear that conversation,' she commented.

The next room was a hospital at Balaklava, where Florence Nightingale was compassionately tending to wounded British soldiers. 'I feel like an intruder,' Nancy whispered to Gayle, staring at the close-packed beds draped with mosquito netting and the tortured men who lay suffering. Florence Nightingale was coolly and efficiently tying a bandage around a soldier's chest. 'I feel like going in to help.'

'Yes, miss,' a voice behind them stated. Startled, the women turned. A tall, tired-looking guide with a long, droopy mustache was standing there. 'Properly done,' he continued in a sad voice, 'the art of the wax figure can be used to create intense emotions in the person viewing the scene. Pity and pride, of course; but also hate, fear, and even love can be engendered by the artist in wax, if he is good at his trade.'

'I think I see what you mean,' Nancy said.

'I've been working here for twenty-eight years, miss, and I've seen grown men break down and cry like babies at what they've seen here. Other times, miss, I've observed persons go into rages over figures or scenes and attack them and attempt to break them up so that they had to be forcibly restrained. Would you like to see the Chamber of Horrors?'

'I don't know whether I could take any horrors today,' Nancy said.

'Oh Nancy, let's do,' Gayle said. 'It will be so much fun.'

'Well . . . '

'I should be privileged to be your guide,' the man offered, 'and see that your sensibilities are not offended by any of the exhibits. Also explaining to you such as you do not understand, and carrying on a running commentary of the facts and stories associated with the scenes.'

'In that case,' Nancy said, 'then by all

means, let us see the Chamber of Horrors.'

The room was large, low-ceilinged, and very poorly lighted. The exhibits were so arranged that each one presented itself suddenly to you as you rounded the corner from the last.

'This is Montressor,' their guide told them as they stood in the front of a man busily walling up a corner of a cellar room, while a second man, chained to the corner, was on his knees pleading to be released. The effect was starkly realistic, from the stagnant pool of water on the cellar floor to the red-eyed rat leering around a brick. 'From a story related by the American author, Edgar Allen Poe.'

'"The Cask of Amontillado",' Nancy whispered, fascinated by the scene.

'You will observe the cask itself in the far corner,' the guide commented. 'Now we come to something a little more home-grown — Edinburgh, to be precise.' He escorted them around the corner. It was the back door of a large brick building. A man had just opened the door and was peering out, bull's-eye lantern in his hand. In the spotlight cast by the lantern, two evil-looking men in ragged clothes, one with a patch over one eye, were carrying the body of a young woman. It looked as if some sort of sinister transaction were being earned out, but Nancy couldn't tell what.

'Burke and Hare!' Gayle exclaimed.

'Aye, miss. Burke and Hare it is. The year of our lord 1828, in Edinburgh, Scotland. That's Burke in front, and Doctor Knox in the doorway. The unfortunate Mary Patterson is slung over Hare's shoulders. They murdered for profit of the meanest sort: to supply bodies for an anatomical dissection class. Under ten pounds a body, they got.'

'I remember,' Gayle said, and recited softly:

'*Up the close and down the stair,*
In the house with Burke and Hare.
Burke's the butcher, Hare's the thief,
Knox the boy that buys the beef.''

'That's the way it goes, miss,' the guide

said. 'That's how they sing it. And Doctor Knox was one of the most respectable medical men in Edinburgh. The villainy of people passes understanding. This way, please.'

The next scene was a pleasant one of a dapper little man drowning his wife in a bathtub. Then they passed on to the Mad Killer of Hamburg, who stood there with a wild gleam in his eye and a butcher knife dripping blood.

'Neither of you young ladies has a delicate constitution what shouldn't be easily shocked, if I may inquire?' the guide asked.

'I don't think I could be too horribly shocked by anything in wax,' Nancy replied.

'Oh do shock us, my man,' Gayle said, clapping her gloved hands together. 'I haven't been shocked in ever so long.'

'As you wish,' the guide said stolidly in his soft voice. 'Please come right this way, ladies.'

A whole corner of the room was taken up by a great display titled 'The French Revolution: The Time of Terror'. In the center of the display, on a raised wooden platform, was the guillotine, its gaunt wooden frame casting a jagged shadow across the crowd of French peasants watching below. Behind the platform the tumbril stood, with its load of aristocrats waiting to feed the gleaming steel triangle that was poised in wait for another neck. The wooden stock had been put in place around the neck of a young richly dressed man who, even kneeling ready for the blade, still glared defiantly out at the crowd. A handsome woman stood between two ragged guards on the platform, to follow her husband to death. The hooded executioner's hand was ready on the release-rope.

'What you see before you,' the guide said, 'was a common sight in Paris during the time of the Terror. The aristocracy of France was being destroyed day by day under the blade of Madame La Guillo-tine, while the peasants stood by and knitted and cheered as each new head fell into the dreadful basket.'

Something about the flickering light brought the whole horrible scene to life, and Nancy and Gayle stood silently before the tragedy of an earlier age. Suddenly, before their eyes, the kneeling figure seemed to jerk and struggle to get free, his face turned to implore the grimacing crowd. Then the executioner pulled the rope, and the gleaming blade dropped free, whistling down its track, until it reached the bottom with a sickening thunk, and a severed head fell into the waiting basket.

Gayle screamed and covered her eyes. Nancy was never sure afterward whether she had screamed or not. For a second she felt faint and dizzy, but then the haze lifted from her eyes and she stared again at the scene. She hadn't imagined it. The great blade was down, and the now-still body had no head.

'It's our finest illusion,' the guide said proudly. 'Strong men have fainted when they've stood where you stand and seen what you just saw.'

'I cannot doubt it,' Nancy said.

'What a horrible thing,' Gayle gasped. 'Horrible.' She slowly uncovered her eyes and stared at the terribly altered display.

'What a horrible thing to show to people.'

'What a horrible thing for people to do to people,' Nancy said.

'Yes, miss,' the guide agreed. 'I have often thought that it is very curious that all of the events shown in this Chamber of Horrors are crimes committed by one person on another. Wolves or tigers, miss, are gentle beasts compared to people. If you've seen enough for today . . . ?'

'I think so,' Nancy whispered.

'I *do* think so,' Gayle said, nodding her head sharply. 'I do.'

'Very good. This way, please.'

And they were out of the Chamber of Horrors. The guide tipped his hat and left them before either Nancy or Gayle had time to dig into her purse for a coin.

'What a strange man,' Nancy said.

'What an awful place,' Gayle responded. 'That was positively shocking. Well, at least this room holds no surprises for us. I don't know whether my constitution could stand it.' The wide hallway they were in was lined with costumed replicas of famous generals and statesmen of the past.

A figure suddenly appeared from a side

door and abruptly disappeared back into it. Nancy gripped Gayle's arm. 'Who was that?' she gasped.

'What?' Gayle started. 'Oh Nancy, don't frighten me like that. One of the attendants, probably. That certainly made you jumpy, didn't it?'

'That must be it,' Nancy said, loosening her grip on Gayle's arm. No use frightening the young woman any further, but she was sure of what she had seen. No mistaking that twisted, ugly face. The man who had so briefly appeared in the hallway had been William, Alan DeWit's servant! What could he have been doing there? Then, as they walked toward the exit, Nancy realized: he must have been the one following them; the passenger of the omnipresent hansom with the yellow horse.

She looked behind when they left, but he was nowhere in sight. Just that one brief glimpse; could she have been mistaken? No — why would anyone else have darted away so rapidly upon seeing them in the hall? It must have been someone with reason to stay hidden from them; and from that one glimpse, she was sure it was William.

Nancy let Lady Gayle off at her town house, some two miles from Benjamin House, and then sank into brooding thought as the carriage brought her home. Why would William have been following them around? Could Alan have some design on her, some plan to harm her while away from the house? Or could he just be trying to keep track of her movements for some unknown reason? It didn't make sense. Certainly if Alan wished to injure — or kill — her, it would be infinitely easier to accomplish within the house that both of them shared. And if he cared where she went, then where was it he wanted her to go — or not to go?

When Nancy returned home, she had her first pleasant surprise: Miss Prudence Walpole was standing in the hall amidst a pile of baggage, busily directing the servants as to its removal.

'Cousin Prudence!' Nancy cried. 'How wonderful to see you!'

'Humph!' Prudence said; but she met

Nancy halfway, and they hugged each other for quite a long time before either could let go.

'We didn't expect you for months yet,' Nancy said breathlessly.

'Sister and I still had nothing to say to each other,' Prudence said. 'Left after a week.'

'Have you heard . . . ?'

'Yes. Don't worry about a thing. I'll take care of him. Robert's always breaking arms or slicing himself open. Thought he outgrew it. Guess not.'

'I must talk to you. Let me go up to my room and change.'

'I'll be up directly,' Prudence said.

Nancy stopped at Robert's room, to find Doctor Moran just coming out. 'Doctor,' she said. 'How is he?'

'It's very encouraging,' Dr. Moran said. 'He's — ah — sleeping now. The coma has broken. But he's still very weak.'

'Let me see him,' she said, going into the room. Robert lay peacefully sleeping on the bed. As she approached, her nose was assaulted by an unpleasant heavy, sweet smell. 'What is that?' she asked.

'What?'

'The aroma?'

'Sickroom smell?' Dr. Moran smiled. He came in beside her and sniffed. 'In this case, it's mostly chloroform. Use it to sterilize the instruments. We're coming more and more to realize the importance of sterility in the medical profession. Sterilize everything these days. Come along, we must let him sleep.'

'Of course, Doctor,' she said, going out and softly closing the door behind her. 'Now that Cousin Prudence is here — Miss Walpole — there'll be someone to watch him all the time, until he gets better.'

'I don't think that will be necessary, young lady,' Dr. Moran said. 'Your brother will be in bed for a while longer, but he'll be all right. He doesn't need constant nursing, or I would have called for a night nurse.'

'I'd feel better, Doctor, if Robert were watched. You can never tell what will happen.' How could she tell him the real reason she was so concerned about her brother lying helpless in bed? It wasn't his health, but his safety she was worried about.

'We'll see, young lady. If it would make you feel better. We'll see what your brother says about it tomorrow; he should be awake by then.'

'That's fair enough, Doctor,' Nancy agreed. She would find some way to convince her brother. She would certainly be able to convince Prudence. Happy for the first time since they arrived at Benjamin House, Nancy went to her room.

8

It couldn't be said that Prudence agreed. On the other hand, Prudence didn't definitely disagree. She merely withheld her opinion. She didn't think that anyone was trying to murder Robert. She did think that Nancy had read entirely too many of those novels as an impressionable child. However, at Nancy's insistence, she was willing to babysit Robert until he recovered. 'Can't never tell,' she sniffed. 'Brain concussion is a tricky thing. Might have convulsions any time. Swallow his tongue and choke. Had a great aunt nearly died that way.' And, on that cheery thought, she went away to unpack and settle into her room.

Meb came upstairs, bringing hot water and towels. 'If you want to take a bath, mum,' she said, 'tub's right across the hall.'

'How long would it take to fill?' Nancy asked.

'Only 'bout five minutes, mum. Hot water's laid on downstairs, and the baron — the last baron, that is — had pipes installed right before he died. Turn on the tap, and hot water comes right out into the tub.'

'Then why do you bring that pitcher up from downstairs?'

'Why, I don't know, now that you mention it, mum. I always have.'

'You must learn to change with the times,' Nancy said. 'Meb, from now on, bring the pitcher up empty and fill it at the tap.'

'Yes, mum.'

'Fine. Now please fill the tub for me.'

'Yes, Miss Nancy.'

Nancy lay in the tub for a long time, playing with the large egg-shaped soap and feeling warm and protected. The bathroom wasn't much larger than the tub, and held nothing else. The walls were tiled, with each separate tile showing a different picture of a rural scene. Nancy stared at cows and sheep and barns and hedge-bound fields until she felt thoroughly bucolic, and then she wrapped herself in a huge terrycloth bath towel, covered herself with a demure bathrobe, and returned to her room.

Nancy rang for Meb and had a tray sent to her room. She didn't feel like dressing for dinner and then sitting down to a large table, to eat all by herself. While she was waiting for the tray, she went down to the library to find something she could read herself to sleep with. She had little hope of finding one of the novels that Prudence disapproved of, but her tastes were catholic: a readable book on any subject would serve.

The library was small, but filled from floor to ceiling with leather-bound books. Nancy, her candle in front of her, peered at the titles. They mostly seemed of one sort — the outdoor world. *A Practical Manual of Field Sports* filled three large volumes. A large book with hand-colored plates proved to be *Equine Anatomy: a Functional Study*. There was *Shot Gunning in the Lowland Marshes*, and *The Compleat Cyclopedae of Sport Gunnery*, and *Powder and Pellet, the Muzzle-Loader's Guide to*

Shotte-Gunning. Colonel Percival Hamilton-Hooker, Lord Benjamin's *Guide to the Hunt* proved to be her great-great-grandfather's privately printed study of the art and science of fox hunting.

Finally Nancy found the small fiction section, and ran her hand gently over the works of Dickens, Jane Austen, Fielding, and Lord Bulwer. She pulled out a copy of Browning's *The Ring and the Book*, and found that it was a first edition, with the pages still uncut. After browsing a bit longer, she finally settled on a copy of *Little Dorrit*, and pulled it from its place on the shelf.

Wedged behind the row of Dickens, as Nancy saw when she removed *Little Dorrit*, was a small black volume that seemed to be quite old. Nancy pried it loose after removing *Posthumous Papers of the Pickwick Club* and *Dombey and Son*. The title proved to be *The Benjamin Legend, an account of the false legend revolving around the Baronecy Benjamin & especially concerning Benjamin House, Shewing how such legends can grow and attain prominency*. It was undated, but appeared to be from the latter part of the eighteenth century.

Nancy took her two prizes and went back upstairs, to find that Meb and her dinner had arrived before. 'Thank you, Meb,' she said. 'That will be all for tonight. You can pick up the tray in the morning.'

'Very good, mum,' Meb said, curtseying and scurrying out the door.

Nancy, who had thought she wasn't hungry, devoured the thick mutton soup, and the chops, and most of the potatoes and vegetables. She retained interest until the pudding, which was some sort of thick, gelatinous, vaguely vanilla-flavoured mess. Putting the tray aside, she got into bed, pulled up the coverlet, and turned her attention to the two books she had brought up from the library. She lay *Little Dorrit* aside for now, in favor of the slim octavo which gave an account of the Benjamin legend.

The pages were well-worn and frequently dog-eared, showing the interest her ancestors had in the same subject.

Only the first few chapters dealt directly with the legend, the rest being an account of how it had spread through England and France, and the elements it had in common with other unverifiable 'buried treasure' stories.

The first chapter, 'What is known of the life and times of the first Baron Benjamin & his relationship with Charles Martyr', Nancy read with interest. She was disappointed to learn that the author concluded that the 'treasure' was almost certainly mythical. She read on:

★   ★   ★

So as we can see, the basis for the legend seems to lie solely in the undoubted fact that Charles I did spend some time in the company of, and at the estate of, his loyal and trusted friend, Sir Thomas Hooker, Baron Benjamin. It can be stated with certainty that, in the few years before his flight to Scotland, Charles I visited the estates of many of his nobility, and, in the last year, certainly over half a hundred.

Then there is the serious question of

whether the king, who had fled north to raise an army to regain his throne, would have left his portable wealth behind — the only means of securing money other than begging from his royal cousins. Would he further have left it in the hands of a known supporter of the royalist cause? Would he have left it close to London, then in the hands of the roundheads, where it might be found by any mob caring to rip down Benjamin House, which, while well-armed and secured, was far from being a moated castle?

The answer to these questions can only be: No.

Then what of the famous Rhyme of the Benjamins? There can only be one answer, which a careful reading and interpretation of the lines will reveal at once:

'Face Second Watch from Benjamin Square'

'Benjamin Square' cannot refer to the so-named intersection in front of Benjamin House, which did not even exist a hundred years ago. It must, therefore, refer to the seat of Benjamin Manor: the chair of the Benjamins. Indeed, I go so far as to suggest that the line first read: 'Face Second Watch from Benjamin Chair.'

In regard to 'Second Watch', the present Baron Benjamin has very kindly allowed me to peruse the daybooks in his possession, which go back to the sixteen-sixties, although not, unfortunately, quite so far back as the time in question. They disclose that the Standing Watch of Benjamin House — at a time when all great houses maintained their own guards, a practice which is in decline today, the liveried staff taking up this reduced function. — was divided into first, second, third, and fourth watch, each responsible for patroling a separate area of the house & grounds. Second Watch was at the north battlement — a feature that still survives on Benjamin House.

Therefore, the instructions in the first line are: from the centre of Benjamin House, face north. Why north? Because that is where Baron Benjamin's Liege Lord, Charles I, is waiting to return.

'Pace out the steps, for you know what is there.'

What is there? Who is there! Charles Martyr.

'Left march when you come about the great ring'

Here we have to enter the realm of conjecture. This is a clear instruction, and we cannot directly know its import. I suggest that the 'great ring' is a ring in the possession of King Charles; possibly the great ruby ring presented to him by Louis XIII upon the occasion of his marriage to Henrietta Maria. When this ring was shown to Baron Benjamin, probably by a secret courier, it would have been a sign that Charles was ready to attempt his return, and that Baron Benjamin was to prepare. As we know, this occasion never arose.

'Out, up, to the left, and return to the King.'

Return to the king indeed. Possibly the reason this rhyme has persisted for a hundred and fifty years, since the need for it has died, is the bitter ache of an unfulfilled trust.'

There the chapter ended. The next chapter took up the appearance of the rumor that a large treasure was hidden somewhere in Benjamin House, and traced it from its origins in London during the Restoration. Nancy read on, fascinated by the story, although a bit disappointed that, in this gentleman's opinion, it was no more than that — a story.

She read of the 'treasure mob' that had camped on the grounds of Benjamin House for a week in June of 1743, defying the efforts of guards and constables to drive them off, and destroying ancient fruit trees and several outbuildings in an attempt to find the treasure; of various people and parties that had attempted to break into the cellar to search; of the crowd that had gathered in 1767 to watch the laborers dig to put in the new road that went by the front gate.

In 1793, the baron — referred to in the book as 'the late baron' — had hired a builder to come in and inspect the cellars in search of possible hiding-places. The man spent six fruitless months at the task, and found exactly nothing. The baron had hoped that this would lay the rumour to rest, but all it succeeded in doing was dividing the believers into two groups: those who thought the treasure was too well hidden for a mere builder to find (Why didn't he hire an architect, then?), and those who now believed that the old baron had indeed found the treasure, and was hiding it in some new spot for his eventual use.

As Nancy was reading, a folded piece of paper suddenly fell from between the pages of the book. She put the book down and unfolded the paper, which proved to have a drawing in pencil on it. For a minute she couldn't make out what it was supposed to be, all boxy and square, with lines and exes and small numbers written in the corners. Then she remembered, and turned back to the page in the book that had an illustration of the builder's rendering of the cellar of Benjamin House. This drawing was a crude copy of that plan. There were lines and marks on the copy that weren't on the original, some of them deeply inscribed and underlined.

Nancy felt a strong sense of the ridiculousness of this discovery. Here was the map of some past treasure hunter concealed in the pages of a book that systematically proved that the treasure had never existed. She wondered how long and how earnestly the hunter — possibly one of her own ancestors — had spent their time in a futile search for the Benjamin treasure.

Nancy examined the map for some time, wondering at the markings on it. Gradually she developed a nagging feeling that there was something about the document that she hadn't realized; some relevant fact that her subconscious had picked up and was trying to make her see. Then, in a flash, she knew what it was: The map was new! Certainly drawn within the past few years, and quite probably more recently than that. The fold lines didn't have the well-scored look of paper that had rested pressed in a book for a great length of time. Although of cheap quality, it was fresh and un-yellowed, and the scribbled notations in ink along the side were still black and bold; though this was no proof by itself, as some ink took years to turn brown, and some never did. But the points all added up to indicate that this map was the quite recent work of someone who was interested in the Benjamin treasure. Someone who had access to the house and library.

Nancy put the book and paper aside and stared, fully awake, at the far wall. She had been reading to put herself to sleep, but now she felt that she wouldn't be able to sleep for some time to come.

Picking up *Little Dorrit,* she tried to read herself to sleep. But sleep refused to come. After a while the letters on the page began to blur and dance around, so she put the book aside and closed her eyes. But she still didn't feel drowsy; her mind went around in a closed loop of wonder and question. Was the book right, and the treasure only a myth? Who had made the map, and why? Could that be part of the motive of whoever was trying to kill her brother — and possibly herself?

Questions without answers only led to more questions, in an endless spiral of frustration and fear. Nancy forced herself to pick up the book again and concentrate on someone else's problems.

A cup of hot chocolate would put her to sleep. She contemplated pulling the bell-pull, but decided she couldn't wake anyone else just for her own indulgence. By now it must be quite late. *A true lady, Nancy reflected, would think nothing of waking five servants for her pleasure. I will have to get in practice — but not tonight.*

It occurred to her that she had never been in the kitchen; but if milk and chocolate were to be found, she supposed she could find them. She put on her robe, slid her feet into a pair of cloth slippers, took her candle, and proceeded downstairs.

The kitchen was, as she assumed it must be, through the far door to the dining room. There was a white-tiled room containing only cupboards and a sink — the butler's pantry, Nancy guessed — and then the kitchen. It was a cheery room, with a large fireplace still holding a bed of red-hot coals. There was a gas stove, with a complex of burners and drafts and switches that made it look capable of running a steam locomotive. Nancy wouldn't have dared try to operate the oven, but she thought she could figure out how to light one burner. *It is better to light one burner,* she thought inanely, taking the box of wooden kitchen matches from its special shelf on the wall, *than to curse the darkness.*

She found the milk-can in the ice-chest, and the chocolate, each square lovingly wrapped in its own paper, on a shelf in the cupboard. It took her a few minutes to find the sugar, which proved to be in a special tin-lined bin built into the cabinets. She scraped two squares of chocolate into a small pot with a slight bit of water and put it on the stove. While she was waiting for it to dissolve and melt, she sweetened the milk and heated it in a separate pan. Then she poured the two together into a pitcher and fixed a small tray.

It was in the butler's pantry that she

heard the noise: a curious sort of throbbing sound that seemed to come from all around. She put down the tray and tried to determine where the sound was coming from. The throbbing stopped, to be almost immediately replaced by a kind of irregular thumping. The sound seemed to come from solid objects, and to be loudest nearer the floor.

The noise was not frightening; it seemed to be caused by some sort of process — digging, building, moving, or something of the sort. It wasn't until Nancy remembered how late at night it was that she became worried. Digging? Where could anyone be digging in the house? Perhaps in the cellars — perhaps it was whoever had drawn that map. Nancy decided that she wasn't going into the cellar alone. Tomorrow, during the day, with Prudence or one of the servants, she would find some excuse to visit them. The diggers wouldn't be there, but there should be some sign of their work.

Having decided that, she picked up the tray and proceeded upstairs. It was in the corridor outside her room that she heard the next sound: a scraping; then a hurried, impatient whisper. This was too much. She put the tray down inside the room; then, leaving her candle behind, she slipped back out into the corridor. She had no definite idea of what she was going to do. It wasn't that Nancy had suddenly become unafraid, but that her curiosity had grown greater than her fear. The candle was left behind for a practical reason: it was much better at causing one to be seen than at aiding one to see.

Nancy slipped down the hall in the dark, running her hand along the wall for guidance. For a minute she didn't hear anything; then faint sounds came down to her from the floor above. She tiptoed up the narrow stairs and into the upstairs hall. There she stood, at the top of the landing, waiting silently. For a long time there was no sound at all, and Nancy got increasingly nervous, alternating between thinking she had imagined it all and being convinced that someone was sneaking up behind her. Then the noises again: footsteps, and the creak of a door. They came from somewhere ahead of her, down a narrow, unfamiliar corridor that led back toward the center of the house, the bar of the U-shape.

Nancy went along in the direction of the sound with one hand resting on the wall and the other groping in front of her. It was pitch-dark, but the retinas of Nancy's eyes, reacting to God knew what stray mote of light or memory of vision or perhaps imagery of their own, conjured up tiny demons that danced just to the side of wherever she looked, and misty ghosts that loomed ahead and were not quite seen.

She came to a turning and stood for a moment, uncertain of which way to go. The noise had ceased and a cold, damp draft blew around her ears and billowed the skirt of her robe. She ended her hesitation by turning toward the draft and going slowly forward. The breeze steadily increased, until it felt like wet fingertips caressing her face. Now she could hear the steady tapping of the rain as it fell on the tiled roof. But the sound she was following had ceased. She stood still and listened, and the rain dripped slowly on her face.

'Damn!' someone said from above her.

'Hush!' someone else commanded urgently.

Nancy stepped forward, and her groping hand came into contact with a ladder. At first she thought it was leaning against the wall, but then she realized that it was built in to the side of the corridor. And the sounds had come from above.

Without pausing to think what she was doing, she started up the ladder. Climbing it, even in the dark, caused no hesitation: she had spent too much of her life climbing into haylofts, and had actually lived for a while in an attic room only reached by a wall-ladder. Had she thought of what she might meet at the top, she might have paused; but after following the sound up one flight of stairs and down two dark halls, she wasn't prepared to stop until she had caught it.

The ladder came out in a small covered shed on the roof of the central building. The gabled roofs of the two wings were a story higher than this one, which was flat and pierced with pipes and chimneys and surrounded by a low embattled wall. This was where the watches had stood in the days when the Barons Benjamin had fought to defend their king, their home, and their beliefs against roundhead soldiers and impassioned mobs.

Nancy stepped off the ladder and stood under the shield of the small shed, which inadequately protected her from the cold drizzle that was falling, cutting off even the light of the stars. Someone else was up here; she could hear the slight sound of motion differentiated from the steady drumming of the rain. She turned her head, trying to ascertain where the sound was coming from. Everything was equally dark, equally forbidding, and equally unlikely. Where would someone hide on this flat roof? What was he doing here? What business had anyone on the roof in the middle of the night in the rain? And what would this person of unknown desire and motive do if he found Nancy spying on him? There were at least two of them up here — partners in some strange rite?

Nancy crouched in a corner of the

three-sided shed, carefully avoiding the open trapdoor, and tried to decide what to do. The sensible thing, she was sure, would be to creep down the ladder as quietly as possible and make her way, mouse-like, back to her own room. But then she would never know who was up here or what they were doing. If only she could manage to see without being seen.

There was another sound! It came from somewhere off to her right. Nancy twisted around and tried to get a view of what was happening there, but it was no use; the night was too black. Wait a second — was that a spot of light? Yes! Someone must be using a hooded lantern!

Nancy crept out of her hiding-place, cautiously heading toward that brief glimpse of light. Then it was gone again. The rain fell directly on her now that she was out of the sheltered overhang, causing her hair to hang limp and wet to her cheeks. Water got in her eyes and ran in large droplets off her nose and chin. Her robe was completely soaked through and clung, wet and cold, to her body. *I'll catch a chill and die*, she thought, *and it will serve me right. This is madness. Whoever is up here must be entirely insane or awfully dedicated to some project.* She tried to imagine a scheme that would necessitate climbing around on a deserted rooftop in the middle of a rainy night, and was unsuccessful.

She came to a row of chimneys and carefully peered over the top. There, on the other side of the chimneys, the dark lantern was resting on the rooftop, its fine beam illuminating a square stand of four small brick chimneys about four yards further along the roof. Between the lantern and the brick chimneys, standing right in the beam, two men were huddled under a square of canvas. Their attention seemed to be focused on the chimneys, but what they were doing Nancy was unable to tell. They seemed to be just standing there, silent and motionless, as though awaiting some great event.

The only event connected with chimneys that Nancy knew of suddenly flashed through her mind, and she fought off an attack of the giggles. She felt a strong urge to stand up and inform the two huddled figures that most people wait for Father Christmas at the other end of the chimney. Somehow she didn't think that the two gentlemen would consider it a bit funny. What were they doing there? She wished they would turn around so that she could see their faces. She was fairly sure that, the way the light was facing, they would be unable to see her even if they were staring right at her. But just as a precaution, she kept herself crouched as low behind the chimneys as she could and still see what was going on.

The trouble was, she decided after she'd been there for five minutes, that nothing was going on. The only thing that had happened since she'd been standing there was that now water was running down the inside of her collar and down her back in a steady flow. She hadn't moved, and the two men hadn't moved. She still had no idea what their business was, and was beginning to seriously wonder what she was doing there herself. There were so many mysteries around Benjamin House, and Nancy hadn't sufficient knowledge to separate the important from the foolish. Supposing these were merely two servants fixing a chimney that had suddenly developed an unbearable leak or dangerous draft? It wasn't as though she knew they were really furtive — they might be, but people wouldn't usually go yelling and stamping around for joy when they had to work on a roof on a rainy night.

But if they were there to fix the roof, why didn't they start? They couldn't be standing there discussing what to do, because Nancy was close enough to hear their conversation, and there hadn't been any. But by that token, if they were up there to do something secret, why didn't they start doing that? It looked like they were just up there to stand in the rain.

Without any warning, without any foreknowledge that it was going to happen, Nancy sneezed. Then she stood there, frozen with fear, as the two men whirled around.

'What the . . . ' One of them picked up the dark lantern and turned its beam around to shine on the chimney behind which Nancy was crouched.

'There's some'un there, sur,' the other said softly. 'Right over there. I sees 'is head.'

'Come on out!' the first said sharply. 'What are you doing there, man?'

Now Nancy did giggle. It was Alan DeWit, and somehow, despite her suspicions, she couldn't be afraid of him in this situation. 'I should have guessed,' she said, standing up. 'It would have to be you.'

'It's Miss Nancy, sur,' Bill said, sounding as amazed as if it had been Father Christmas.

'So I notice,' Alan said. 'Miss Nancy, you must be freezing. Here, let me give you my coat.' He came quickly around the chimney barrier, unbuttoning his rubber raincoat. No question about what she had been doing there: the man seemed immune to surprise.

'I heard a noise,' Nancy said lamely, accepting the coat that he wrapped around her. All of a sudden she was freezing. Now that her intense concentration was gone, her teeth were chattering and she realized she was chilled to the bone.

'I shall have to be more careful about the noises I make,' Alan said, 'or we'll have you leaping off the roof. Come. Bill, let's take Miss Nancy inside. I think we've all been out here long enough.'

They helped her down the ladder and escorted her to her room, where they left her to dry off and change. Not having another robe, she pulled on a dry house-dress and took Alan's raincoat and her tray of cold cocoa downstairs.

Alan was waiting for her in the breakfast room. He had managed to dry himself, and looked as neat and elegant as ever in a smoking jacket. 'I can't seem to get this pipe to draw properly,' he said, waving the thin-stemmed problem at her as she came in. 'William will be here in a second with tea — best thing for you when you have a chill. You don't mind the smell of pipe tobacco, do you? I feel that when one is wearing a smoking jacket, one has a moral obligation to smoke.'

'It depends upon the tobacco,' she said. 'I assume you have good taste.'

'Abominable,' Alan said, laughing, and he continued the attempt to light his pipe.

Nancy tried to picture this bright young man in front of her as a villain, and found that she couldn't. But someone had dropped that stone on her brother. William had been following them around in the wax museum — and he had been doing something up on the roof.

'What on earth were you doing on the roof?' Nancy forced herself to ask the question lightly.

Alan considered the question. 'I went up to look at the stars, particularly the Perseids.'

'But it was completely overcast.'

'I know.' Alan sounded sad. 'There was to have been a meteor shower. What a shame to have missed it.'

William arrived with the tea and Alan poured, while Nancy considered this. The answer made no sense whatever. But nothing she could think of made any sense whatever. There was no reason for anyone to be huddled under a canvas at night, in the rain, on a deserted rooftop.

'How is your dart-throwing coming?' Nancy asked.

'Top form,' Alan answered cheerfully. 'I might yet become all-Britain blindfold darts champion. And if anyone leaps out at me from second-floor doorways, I shall be able to handle that, too. I've perfected my catch. Overhand is too strenuous, so I now use the scoop — my own variant.'

Nancy could think of nothing to say, so she sipped her tea. The night's adventures seemed over, and she knew no more than before. Indeed, there were now more questions. Suddenly feeling very tired, Nancy excused herself and went upstairs. She was asleep almost immediately.

9

Robert was awake! And that was glad tidings to get up to on this beautiful morning. Nancy rose as soon as Prudence came in with the news and, throwing open the window to the bright, chill day, hurriedly dressed. All trace of last night's rain had been wiped from the sky, which was a firm, deep blue, holding the great golden orb of the morning sun.

Nancy ran down the hall to her brother's room as soon as she was decently dressed. Prudence and Dr. Moran were already there, and Robert was sitting up in bed, his back propped by two pillows, drinking a cup of broth.

'Robert!' Nancy cried, coming around to the side of the bed and embracing him; trying to be happy and loving and gentle because of his wounds and careful of the cup of broth all at the same time. 'How wonderful to see you again.'

'Hello, Nancy dear,' Robert said,

embracing her with his free hand — the one that wasn't holding the broth. 'I understood that you saw a lot of me while I was unconscious. Doctor Moran says he couldn't keep you out of here.'

'He exaggerates,' Nancy said. 'And besides, you know quite well what I mean.'

'Of course. And I shouldn't fight with you until I get my strength up.'

'How are you?' Nancy asked. 'How is he, Doctor Moran?'

'I'm fine,' Robert said.

'Fine, fine,' Dr. Moran echoed. 'As well as, if not better than, can be expected. Aside from the blow itself, a glancing blow from one of the fragments, Lord Robert seems to have suffered no ill effects. Very lucky. He'll be confined to his bed for a while longer of course, but after that he'll be as fit as a fiddle.'

'Humph,' Prudence sniffed. Nancy, who after long association with their cousin could almost read her mind, knew that she was repressing the urge to ask the good doctor just what was so particularly fit about a fiddle.

'Are you sure I have to stay in bed, Doctor?' Robert asked. 'I feel fine now. A bit dizzy, perhaps, but surely I could — '

'I won't be responsible, milord, for the consequences if you should arise now. A concussion, even a minor one such as you suffered, is a serious thing. You are to stay in bed for the next week. After that you should be fine, but you need that rest. What with the blow to your head and the loss of all that blood, we'd probably have to carry you back to the bed if you did get up.'

'I'll be right here to look after you,' Prudence said after a sniff and a glance at Nancy. 'Just like I always did when you were a boy falling out of trees and picking fights with animals a good bit larger than yourself.'

'You mean that bull,' Robert said. 'Cousin, I was only nine years old; and, as I've told you once a month since then, I honestly didn't know he was there. Aren't you ever going to let me forget that?'

'Humph!' Prudence pulled out her spectacles and adjusted them on her nose. 'How two tons of Hereford bull can manage to sneak up on you in an open pasture is beyond my understanding.'

'Let us reach an agreement,' Robert suggested. 'If you don't talk about it anymore, I won't either.'

'Humph!' Prudence said.

'I'm hungry!' Robert suddenly announced. 'This broth isn't beginning to fill me up. Can't I get some decent breakfast?'

Prudence glanced at Dr. Moran, who nodded approval, and then she got up and stalked out of the room.

'Oh dear,' Nancy said. 'She's gone to get breakfast for you. The servants will disown us.'

'The servants will just have to get used to Prudence,' Robert said. 'And, I imagine, she to them. What sort of servants do we have?'

Nancy giggled. 'Not nearly enough.'

Robert stared at her. 'Fenton, the butler, insists that the house is horribly understaffed,' she explained. 'He and Mrs. Toby — she's the housekeeper — are going to see to that. I've given them permission to hire, subject to your approval of course.'

Robert waved weakly. 'I leave it in your tiny capable hands.'

Dr. Moran excused himself to return to his laboratory, stating firmly that he'd be back at lunchtime, and Robert had better still be in bed.

'You'll like Fenton,' Nancy told Robert. 'He's perfect. Ever so much more upper-class and aristocratic than you or I shall ever be.'

'I shall send him out to all social functions in my place,' Robert declared. 'What about the rest of this skeleton staff?'

Nancy told him about Piggins and Meb and Cook. 'That's the name on her birth certificate, I'm sure of it. She was born 'Cook'.' And Alice and Jane and Little Dwiggens — 'looks like a frightened fawn' — and Messrs. Burke and Pitt; the White Rabbit and Tweedledum. 'And we have a coachman named Boswell, who's recuperating from an illness Fenton will not discuss with a lady.'

'A fertile field for speculation,' Robert commented. Nancy then told him of the Dowager Duchess of Llewelyn and Lady

Gayle, and her shopping trip, and Madame Tussaud and Sons' Waxworks Museum.

'You've made a friend already,' Robert said, smiling and holding her hand. 'I'm glad. I was worried about your facing up to all this while I was lying here. It was quite a shock to wake up this morning — it was still dark — and find myself bandaged all over and lying in a strange bed.'

'But surely it couldn't have been too shocking,' Nancy said. 'After all, getting hit like that, you surely must have understood the bandages.'

'That's it, you see. I don't remember the accident at all.'

'You don't?'

'No. The last thing I remember is getting in the coach to come here. Everything after that is a blank.'

'Oh, Robert! Did you tell Dr. Moran?'

'Yes. He assures me that it's completely normal, even usual. I probably never will remember it, he says. Have you seen that laboratory of his yet? What sort of work does he do in there?'

'I have no idea. That's one part of the house I haven't yet reached in my exploring, and I tell you I have explored some odd areas. Robert, I forgot — did you know there's a man living here?'

'Several, from what you tell me.'

'No, I don't mean the servants. A guest, or boarder, or something. Alan DeWit. Lord Alan, although he doesn't use the title. He had a fight with his family, and Lord DeWit of DeWit kicked him out. The last baron, the one who got kicked by a horse, invited him to stay here, and he's been here ever since. He's . . . strange.' Nancy had been about to rush on and tell Robert about her suspicions, but she decided that this wasn't the time. And besides, they weren't any too clear in her own head.

'What do you mean, strange?' Robert asked,

'Oh, just that he does strange things: plays darts in the dark, and leaps about on the roof, and things.'

'Leaps about . . . ?'

'Well, actually he wasn't leaping about. Standing very still, as a matter of fact.'

'There, you see?' Robert leaned back, smiling. 'You have an imagination that would founder a horse. Leaps about!'

'Well, it was night-time,' Nancy said defensively.

'What were you doing up on the roof at nighttime?' Robert demanded.

'I heard a noise.'

'Well. I shall see about this Alan DeWit as soon as I get on my feet.'

'He offered to move,' Nancy said. 'I told him to wait until we got more organized. I didn't feel right about kicking someone out who's lived here longer than I, and besides I had no right to say anything.'

Robert raised his right hand in a gesture of benediction. 'By the power vested in me by, I guess, Charles the First, I hereby give you the right to say anything you choose. I do this in the firm conviction that you will anyway.' He let his hand drop. 'We'll leave things in the status quo for the next week, then we'll see about servants and guests and things.'

Prudence came in with a sniff and a tray, which she set on Robert's lap.

'Food!' Robert said. 'Even the smell is nourishing.'

'No oatmeal,' Prudence said. 'Said they don't eat it here. Civilized country, and they can't even come up with a civilized breakfast. Fish! Would you believe? Coffee's good. Thought I'd have to settle for tea, from what I heard. Eat your breakfast.'

'Yes, Cousin Pru,' Robert said meekly.

Nancy left Robert and went down to her own breakfast. *Should I tell Robert?* she thought over the poached egg. *No, the question is: What exactly should I tell Robert? That I suspect someone is deliberately trying to kill him? That it may be Alan DeWit?* She decided miserably that she didn't know enough to tell Robert anything. When he was stronger, when she had more information and more time to sort out the meaning of what she did know, then she would go to Robert and explain everything. Whatever 'everything' might turn out to be.

She was sitting over her coffee, her thoughts going in the same circular path, when Fenton came into the breakfast room. 'A note, miss,' he said, and lowered the great silver tray he was carrying to where she could see over the rim. There was a small note, folded and sealed with a huge blob of wax, in the exact center of the tray.

'Thank you, Fenton,' she said, taking the note.

He bowed and took two precise steps backward. 'The messenger awaits without,' he said.

The seal impressed on the wax was an ornate lozenge. Nancy knew enough about heraldry to recognize this as the device that held a woman's arms, rather than the more masculine, military shape of a shield. She stared at the note for a minute, then decided it was silly to speculate about it when it was in her hands for the opening. The seal was so pretty that she hated to break it, so she slid a butter knife under it and opened it with only slight damage to the seal.

The same arms were embossed on the notepaper, and underneath: Lady Elisabeth Gayle Llewelyn, Bratteltum.

The Honourable Miss Nancy Hooker
(the note read)
Benjamin Hall Marylebone

Dear Nancy,
If you are receiving in the forenoon, it would be my pleasure to make a visit.
Do say yes.

Gayle

Nancy seemed to have found a friend. She was glad: she liked Gayle and she was pleased that Gayle seemed to like her; at least enough to repeat the visit. She looked around for a means to reply, and there was Fenton at her elbow with a pen, a small silver inkstand, some notepaper, and a square of blotting paper. 'Thank you,' she said automatically as he arranged these items in front of her, ringing for a maid to clear away the appropriate dishes.

The notepaper bore the Benjamin arms at the top; the same device that was on the carriage door. She examined it closely for the first time. The shield was divided into four parts: the upper left and lower right quadrants each showed a golden chess-castle on a red field. The upper right bore a silver sword hilt down on a blue field. The remaining quarter had three gold lions on a red background.

'This is the Benjamin crest?' she asked Fenton.

'Yes, miss,' Fenton replied, as proudly as if it had been his own (and by now, Nancy supposed, in a sense it was). 'The Benjamin device; quarterly: first and fourth, gules, a rook, or; second, azure, a sword, argent; third, England. It was awarded, so I understand, by Charles the First himself. That being the proper description of it in heraldic terms. For yourself, being a lady, it properly should be in a lozenge. But the last baron was unmarried, and we don't have any feminine notepaper to hand.' He sounded embarrassed. 'I shall see to it that this is remedied at the earliest convenience.'

'That's all right, Fenton. Thank you. I shall make do with masculine notepaper.' She dipped the pen and began:

Lady Elisabeth Gayle Llewelyn
(What was the name of their town-house? Oh, well.)
London

Dear Gayle,
(Now what is the proper form? Is there a book of etiquette about? Well, a friend is a friend!)
Please come.

Nancy.

She folded the note neatly and handed it to Fenton. 'Please give this to the messenger.'

'Yes, miss.' But Fenton wasn't done with it yet. He produced a thin stick of gold sealing-wax, which he heated in a candle flame. At just the right moment he gave it a twist, and a neat-sized drop fell on the fold. Then he reverently produced a brass seal and pressed it — just so — into the wax. Appearance was everything, and Fenton knew it. He gathered the paraphernalia, bowed, and left.

Sir Andrew Dean came in to the

breakfast room long enough to say hello. 'Must get upstairs to speak with Lord Benjamin. Glad he's recovered. Never doubted it. Papers for him to sign; business matters, very dull. I won't stay long. Save anything controversial until he's on his feet. Bad to excite a convalescent. I plan to speak with him concerning getting a telephone; do you think that would excite him?'

Nancy smiled. 'I don't think so. It would probably interest him very much.'

'It should, it should. Coming thing. Pretty soon there'll be one in every home. Duchess Llewelyn was very impressed. Must get upstairs now.' Since Sir Andrew was in such a hurry to go, he only stood in the doorway talking for another five minutes before he excused himself and actually walked away.

Nancy shortly went upstairs herself and changed to meet Lady Gayle. She reflected that she and Gayle seemed to complement each other very well; where one was weak, the other was strong; where one was childlike, the other was adult. It could be the basis for a strong friendship. Nancy hoped so; she liked Gayle, and she certainly needed a friend.

She stopped at Robert's door on the way downstairs, but she could hear her brother and Sir Andrew talking and decided not to disturb them. She continued downstairs and walked down the great corridor toward the rear of the house. The hall would have served as a respectable museum back in Boston: it was a progression of relics and antiques from the late Renaissance to the present. There were paintings and tapestries on the walls that dated from all periods. A row of straight-backed Louis XIV chairs were evenly spaced down the corridor. Suits of armor, from chain mail to full plate, stood on display by the sides of most of the doors. A fan of halberds, flanked by two fans of broadswords, occupied a clear space on the wall. Antique, or merely ancient, chests, tables, and desks took up the empty spots along the wall. Except for the portiere curtains on the windows at the end of the hall, the influence of Queen Victoria and the modern age was completely lacking in the decoration of the corridor. Nancy found the furnishings, ranging in design and construction from the stark to the rich simplicity of the later Louis, very pleasing to her eye. Some of the pieces reminded her of the Colonial furniture she was so fond of, that was so out of style now.

She paused to admire some of the pieces, to run her hand over the wood, rubbed smooth by centuries of polishing. She opened an occasional drawer, to see what forgotten secrets of a past age might lie within. Somehow she felt guilty doing so, and was glad there was no one to see her. She found carefully folded quilts, blankets, and stiff canvas over-garments in one drawer that she couldn't identify a use for.

She stopped at a suit of armor guarding a closed door. It was particularly ornate, with what looked like gold inlay over the breastplate and a helmet of a peculiar design with a peaked top and a sharply pointed visor. Nancy wondered what women wore when the men were prancing around in seventy pounds of sheet iron.

There were voices coming from within the closed door. Nancy at first couldn't hear what they were saying, and wasn't particularly trying to. Then one of the voices came through loud and clear: 'It's even more important now! You mustn't slip up.'

It was Alan! No mistaking that clipped superior speech. Nancy moved closer to the door, now definitely interested in the conversation. The answer was a mumble that she couldn't make out.

Then Alan's voice again: 'No, of course not. Take care not to let her know. That's very important'

Mumble.

'See that you do. I'm counting on you. You haven't failed me yet, and this is no time to start!'

Mumble.

'Yes. It's a shame they had to come now. If only they'd stayed in America for another month. It made what happened inevitable. Nancy's such a nice woman, too — I could be very fond of her.'

His voice was getting louder, as though he were approaching the door. Nancy jumped back with a start and hurried on down the hall. A door across the way was open, and she darted into it.

'Well, Miss Nancy, how nice to see you.' It was Dr. Moran, sitting behind a large desk in the room. A young, meticulously garbed gentleman was in an easy chair to the side of the desk. They both rose as she entered the room. 'Nothing has happened to Lord Robert, I trust?' Dr. Moran asked.

'No, nothing,' Nancy assured him. 'I had some time before my engagement, and I, ah, thought I'd drop in and see this laboratory of yours that I've heard so much about. That is, if you're not busy.'

'No, no, not at all,' Dr. Moran said hastily. 'Miss Nancy, allow me to present Lord Bryce, an old and valued friend of mine. Lord Bryce, Miss Nancy Hooker.'

'Not all that old, I assure you,' Lord Bryce said, extending his hand. And indeed, he didn't look much over thirty. Nancy took his hand and he moved it stiffly up and down twice in a pump-handle ritual. 'Glad to meet you, don't you know. Been planning to drop in and introduce myself as soon as Baron Benjamin was sufficiently recovered. Old friend of the family, you know.' He laughed self-consciously. 'There I go, being old again. It is a pleasure to meet you, Miss Nancy. Jolly good, don't you know.'

Here was the first Englishman Nancy had met who spoke the way Englishmen did on the stage back home. She was intrigued. 'A pleasure, Lord Bryce. You were friends with the late Lord Benjamin?' she asked him, as much to keep him talking as anything else.

He didn't disappoint her. 'Deucedly close to old Johnny,' he told her. 'Hunted together all the time. Tally-ho! Chase the old fox down. Jolly great sport. Deuced fine rider too, Johnny was. Good seat. Only thrown once in his life that I know of, and that was it. Bad show.'

Nancy found his conversation faintly ridiculous, but there was nothing ridiculous about the man. There was a feeling of power and determination in his stance and steady gaze. He was someone who was clearly used to getting what he wanted from life and from the people around him.

'You are a very pretty and charming woman, Miss Nancy,' he said. 'If the climate or whatever of America is responsible for this fine a product, I shall have to jolly well make a pilgrimage.'

Dr. Moran laughed while Nancy was still trying to make up her mind whether to feel pleased or insulted. 'Don't mind Lord Bryce, Miss Nancy; he's a bit forward. Come, let me show you my laboratory. Do you know anything about the science of chemistry?'

'I'm afraid I don't,' Nancy admitted. 'The only science we had in school was astronomy, and that was only because the principal had a telescope set up on the roof of the school.'

'I see, yes. Come through here, and I'll show you what I am engaged in.' He led her through a door at the rear of his small office, and Lord Bryce followed along behind looking politely disinterested.

'The science of chemistry is the oldest in the civilized world,' Dr. Moran lectured as they entered a long room full of exotic-looking glassware and bottles of varicolored liquids and powders. 'It was originally known as alchemy, and was practiced as a mystic rite and secret art by specially trained adepts who considered themselves magicians. It was then principally concerned with transmuting the base metals into gold, and the discovery of the fabled philosopher's stone, reputed to embody among its properties omniscience and immortality. Certainly, you will admit, a goal worth striving for.'

'It would seem so,' Nancy admitted, walking over to admire the equipment. A long center table held a row of coils, tubes, beakers, alcohol lamps, retorts, and binding clips and clamps, all put together in a manner that suggested that they interacted in some way with one another.

'Be careful,' Dr. Moran warned. 'Don't touch anything; it might be dangerous. I use both volatile and poisonous liquids in my experiments.'

'I won't touch anything without inquiring first,' Nancy assured him. She looked closely at the assemblage of glassware, trying to make some sense of the way it was hooked together.

'This, ah, interests you?' Lord Bryce asked. 'I mean, you know, I can't make head nor tail out of it.'

'It's fascinating,' Nancy said, 'but I confess I don't understand it either.'

'I'm afraid it looks more complex than it is,' Dr. Moran said. 'I am running a series of experiments to determine which elements, or combinations of elements, are essential to life. Also in what amounts. It is a curious fact that many elements, which in small amounts are necessary to the life-processes, are, in larger amounts, dangerous or fatal. You do know what an element is?'

'In a vague, general sort of way,' Nancy confessed.

'There are several excellent texts on the subject,' Dr. Moran said with the enthusiasm of a specialist. 'I would be pleased to procure one for you. When you once understand the basics of the subject, you would find it fascinating, and I could better explain to you just what I am doing here.'

'I shall consider your offer,' Nancy

assured him. 'And I thank you for making it.' She was surprised to find herself speaking in the same slightly stilted English as the Doctor. *It must be catching,* she thought. 'I also thank you for taking the time to show this to me. I'll have to come back soon and let you explain it to me in detail.'

'I should be delighted.'

'A pleasure meeting you, Lord Bryce,' Nancy said.

He took her hand. 'Pity you have to leave so soon. I hope to have the chance of getting to know you better — much better.'

'Thank you,' Nancy said, wondering just what he meant by that. She disengaged her hand and excused herself.

When Lady Gayle arrived, Nancy took her upstairs to meet Robert and Prudence, who was sniffing quietly in the corner. 'It is such a pleasure to meet you,' Gayle said. 'Nancy has told me so much about you that I feel I know you already. It's good to see that you're well on your way to recovering from that nasty blow. I do hope you'll like it here in London. I'm sure you will; there's so much to see and do. I shall be delighted to show you and Nancy around London and to introduce you to the proper people and, I suppose, to some of the improper people. Grandmama, the Duchess of Llewelyn, is anxious to make your acquaintance, too. Sir Andrew Dean spoke very well of you to her, but Grandmama says to assure you that she is prepared to think well of you despite Sir Andrew's recommendation. Grandmama is like that.'

Robert was propped up in bed by a motley collection of pillows, and surrounded by books and newspapers. 'I am pleased to meet you,' he said to Lady Gayle, 'and I thank you for your kindness to Nancy. I'm looking forward to making the acquaintance of the Duchess of Llewelyn. Sir Andrew has also told me of her. Has she decided to install a telephone in her house?'

'Grandmama has not decided yet. It seems that the only people you can contact with the telephone are others who have had the apparatus installed. She is having Sir Andrew ascertain whether there is anyone now on the service to whom she would like to talk. Most of those now using the telephone service would appear to be tradesmen; and, as a consequence of this, Grandmama feels that the device would be more properly installed in the servants' quarters. Grandfather, the late duke, refused to accept letters that were sealed with glue instead of sealing-wax; he thought it was vulgar.'

'Gayle,' Nancy said, cutting off the flow of conversation, 'we really should leave now, and let my brother rest.'

'Certainly, of course,' Lady Gayle said. 'I understand. I hope I haven't exhausted him with my chatter. I shall return when you are feeling better, Lord Benjamin.'

'Certainly, Lady Gayle,' Robert said. 'You will always be welcome.'

The women had gone downstairs and were preparing to go out for a drive when Lord Bryce came hurrying up from the rear of the house. 'Miss Nancy,' he boomed, 'how lucky that I could catch you — Good day, Lady Gayle — before either of us left for the day. I had a rather striking idea — at least, I hope you'll think so — and I wished to convey it to you. You see, I have these tickets for Covent Garden tonight — a box, don't you know, to see *Idomeneo.*'

'*Idomeneo?*'

'It's an opera. Mozart. First run. I was to take my Aunt Dee and Cousin Clothile, but Cousin Clothile has come down with the withers or yaws or something, and is determined to be incapacitated tonight. So I have this extra ticket, and I was wondering if you . . . I mean, that's not the right way to ask, but dash it all . . . Look here, will you come with me tonight? My aunt will be along, so we'll be properly chaperoned.'

He didn't look so positive as he had when they had met earlier. Indeed, he looked like a panting sheepdog, waiting for its master to throw it a bone. Nancy turned to look at Gayle, but could read nothing in the expression on her face. 'I've never been to an opera,' Nancy said contemplatively.

'Good, then it's settled!' Lord Bryce said. 'I shall pick you up at eight. Must run now. Cheerie-ho. Nice speaking to you, Lady Gayle.' And he was out the front door.

'Yes indeed,' Lady Gayle snapped to his retreating back. 'Wonderful conversation we had.'

'Gayle!' Nancy said. 'Don't you like him?' The horrible thought came to her that perhaps Gayle did like him very much, and was hurt by his inviting Nancy out. The fact that what he had evidently taken for acceptance hadn't been meant that way didn't help.

'Lord Bryce?' Lady Gayle shrugged her shoulders in an affectedly dainty manner. 'He is but a toad.'

'Oh,' Nancy said, wondering what that meant. 'Is that bad? Should I refuse to go out with him? I could develop a headache or break an arm or something.'

'The lecturer that I heard last month,' Gayle said, taking Nancy by the arm, 'who insisted that man was above the animals because he replaced instinct with reason, must be mistaken. I feel an instinctive dislike of that man. That's no reason to refuse his offer, you understand. Are you ready to go out? When one is invited to the opera, properly chaperoned, one should go to the opera. Have you anything to wear?'

'No. That is, I don't believe so. What does one wear to the opera?'

'Something elegant. Something one has never worn before. One goes to the opera as much to be seen as to see. I tell you what — we shall go over to my house, and I shall loan you a superior gown.'

Nancy thanked Gayle and agreed. First she went up to get her brother's approval of the proposed evening. He gave it tentatively, subject to Dr. Moran's vouching for the young man. Nancy had to smile at this. *Robert's being all stuffy and fatherly,* she thought. And somehow she couldn't picture Lord Bryce as a 'young man', although he was certainly not very old.

Dr. Moran verified that Lord Bryce was of an excellent family; and, although that wasn't what Robert was asking, he settled for that and agreed to allow Nancy her evening.

Lady Gayle's closet was impressively full of gowns suitable for wear at an opera, or indeed anything up to a coronation. Nancy stood in front of a full-length mirror, holding silk brocades and moires and satins in front of her, loving each new gown more than the last and totally unable to make up her mind.

'I do believe,' Gayle said finally from the chair where she had been watching Nancy with a critical eye, 'that you would look fine in any of them, and we do seem to be of about the same size. But I think you should settle for something warmer than silk, as the nights are chill and Covent Garden is scarcely adequately heated.'

They finally settled on a golden-brown English cashmere gown with puff sleeves, ruffled shoulders and a wide, full skirt. Gayle completed the outfit by supplying a tan cape with a red silk lining and ruffled collar, and red lace ornamentation and edgings.

'I shall be elegant!' Nancy cried, pirouetting as she held the dress.

'Superior,' Gayle agreed.

'Oh Gayle, you should tell me: what is it that you dislike about Lord Bryce?'

'It's hard to say.' Gayle shrugged elaborately. 'I don't know him well, and I know nothing against him. His family is good. He has exemplary manners, but I've always felt that he wore them as a sort of bib — to be removed at will, rather than as a part of him, if you see what I mean.'

'I think I do.'

'Don't let that stop you from enjoying yourself this evening,' Gayle insisted. 'It's only my opinion, you know. And besides, one must go out with all sorts of men if one is to gather experience in life and be a well-rounded person.'

'I think I should be content to be insufficiently rounded in some areas of experience,' Nancy said.

'You should go now. Be sure to tell me all about it tomorrow!'

'I shall,' Nancy assured her. 'Gayle, thank you for the gown — and everything.'

'It's my pleasure. Here, let's pack that carefully.' Gayle rang for the maid and sent the garments off with her to be boxed for the short trip back to Benjamin

159

House. 'Remember, don't be overawed by anything. Look superior and condescending and faintly amused. Being faintly amused is all the rage now; last year it was unutterable boredom. One must keep one's emotions fashionable.'

'I'll do my best not to fail you,' Nancy said. 'Goodbye.' She left the building and climbed back in the Llewelyn coach.

'*Au revoir!*' Gayle waved from the doorway, looking superior, condescending, and faintly amused.

Nancy found that the prospect of going out for the evening was strangely exciting and unnerving. She was neither drawn to nor repelled by Lord Bryce, and resolved to let her opinion of him be formed as the evening progressed. But this was her first night out in London, as well as her first opera. It would certainly be one she would long remember.

When she arrived home, Nancy first soaked in a hot tub, staying immersed until she felt glowingly clean, relaxed, and calm. Then she put on a robe, and Meb helped her with the curling iron, heating and pressing until her hair was a perfectly waved halo around her head and falling down to her shoulders.

'Very nice, Miss,' Meb said finally. 'Here, let me brush it out for you in back. That's right. Now, where's that tortoise comb? Ah! Now, a little bit more — around the right side, like that — and across here — there! Now look at yourself, Miss Nancy — here, use the hand mirror. What do you think?'

Nancy stared at her double reflection, from the vanity mirror to the hand mirror, and slowly turned her head from side to side. Meb had rearranged her hair only slightly from the way she usually wore it. The difference was subtle, almost unnoticeable, but it made her look somehow both more sophisticated and more alive. 'Why, Meb, this is excellent,' she said. 'Wherever did you learn to handle a comb and brush like that?'

'Thank you, miss. The last situation I held was with Lady St. Simon, and she was particularly fastidious about such things. She taught me a lot.'

'I see,' said Nancy, wondering whether Meb thought her to be unfastidious about such things. 'At any rate, you've done very well, and I commend you. Thank you, Meb.'

'I'm glad you're pleased, Miss Nancy,' Meb said, looking pleased herself.

Nancy sent downstairs for a sandwich while she finished dressing. The dress fit almost perfectly, and as soon as Meb had basted up the hem it looked like it had been made for her.

The sandwich tray arrived while she was pondering the question of jewelry. Not that she had that wide a choice: the items in her jewel box were the few tilings she had inherited from her mother, and a brooch her father had given her on her sixteenth birthday.

'Here you are, mum,' Meb said, setting the tray down. 'Cook fixed you a cup of good broth to go with the sandwiches. My, don't you look elegant, Miss Nancy!'

'Thank you, Meb,' Nancy said, wishing that Meb hadn't sounded quite so surprised at her looking 'elegant'. Both the broth and the tea, steeping in a dainty porcelain pot, were too hot for her to drink, so she concentrated on the sandwiches. There were two: a hard cheese and a sort of meatloaf, on crustless home-baked bread. She hadn't realized how hungry she was until she started eating. It wasn't until the last half of the last sandwich was about half-gone that she stopped. For Nancy, who always had a light appetite, this was a heavy meal. She sipped at the broth and drank a cup of tea before deciding she was finished.

She had decided on a pearl ring set in a thin gold band that had been her mother's, and her father's twined-gold brooch. Since she couldn't be glitteringly ornate, she would be classically simple.

She regarded the final result in the vanity mirror. 'I shall have to get a full-length looking-glass,' she said to Meb as she twisted back and forth and bobbed up and down to get a feeling of the total effect.

'Yes'm,' Meb agreed. 'You do look elegant.' She sounded more positive and less surprised this time, as though she had grown quite used to the idea.

'Thank you again, Meb,' Nancy said. 'With your help, we'll try to keep it this way. It wouldn't do to disgrace the name of Benjamin by having an inelegant-looking mistress in the house.'

'No'm,' Meb said, obviously not sure of what she was agreeing to.

Nancy made a few final adjustments, and then picked up her cape. 'Would you please take my wrap downstairs,' she said, handing it to Meb. 'I want to stop in at my brother's room.'

'Yes, Miss Nancy,' Meb said, and left with the dinner tray and cape.

Nancy went down to her brother's room and knocked on the door.

'Come in!' Robert called. She entered, to find Alan DeWit sitting by the side of the bed. The two men had obviously been deep in conversation, but it broke off as she came in.

Alan rose. 'Miss Hooker,' he said. 'What a pleasure to see you. And I must say you're looking exceptionally radiant tonight.

'*Small is the worth*
Of beauty from the light retir'd;
Bid her come forth,

164

Suffer'd herself to be desir'd,
And not blush so to be admir'd.''

'Why, thank you, Mr. DeWit,' Nancy said, afraid that she was blushing.

Alan smiled. 'I didn't mean to embarrass you. It sprang, uncalled-for, from my heart.'

'Nice bit of poetry, Alan,' Robert said, looking quizzically at his visitor.

'Not my own, I assure you. From the vast resources of a public-school education, that enable one to seem clever with memorized wit. Fellow named Waller wrote it some two hundred years ago, to a lady named Lucy Sidney. I would endeavor to write a poem to you, my dear Nancy, were it not for the fear of showing myself for the commonplace, incapable dolt that I am. No, I'm afraid I shall regale you only with other people's words, like poor Christian in *Cyrano de Bergerac*.' He smiled and gave a half-bow, leaving Nancy wondering how much of what he said had been serious, and what she should take it to mean.

Suddenly she remembered: this was the

man she suspected of attempting to kill Robert! When he was around, her suspicions fled. The man was charming, and she must watch out for that. But was the charm any deeper a part of him than the tweed jacket he was wearing with such casual elegance? She had racked her mind for another solution; but however she turned the problem, it still came up murder. Once failed, but there was nothing to stop him from trying again. And he was deeply a part of whatever mysterious happenings were going on in this house at night, perhaps supplying the motive for the attempt. What could he be speaking to Robert about? Was this part of some second plan to make up for the first failure? She would have to warn her brother; tell him of what was happening. No matter how silly he thought her, she must convince him to take precautions.

Should she stay home tonight; make some excuse not to go to the opera? No — Robert was surely safe until after the servants retired, and she would be home by then. She would speak to him as soon as she returned. Nancy bit her lip; now she was going to spend the whole evening worrying, and not enjoying the opera and the company of Lord Bryce.

Robert stared at her, as ever able to read her moods. 'Is something wrong, Nancy?'

'No,' she assured him. 'Nothing.'

'Don't worry,' he said. 'You look beautiful. Just go out and enjoy yourself.'

Robert thought she was worried about the opera, as if that mattered. Nancy scarcely remembered how nervous she had been a few hours before. The only thing that mattered now was to somehow get through the evening and come home to find Robert still safe. 'I do expect to enjoy myself,' she said. 'Thank you. Take care. It was nice speaking to you, Mr. DeWit.'

★   ★   ★

Lord Bryce and his aunt arrived fifteen minutes early. Nancy, obeying Gayle's strict instructions as to how a lady must behave, kept them waiting in the front room for ten minutes before she came down. 'Terribly sorry to have kept you waiting,' she said, sailing into the room. 'Meb! Bring my wrap, please.'

'Quite all right, I assure you,' Lord Bryce said. 'Miss Nancy Hooker-Benjamin, may I present my aunt, Miss Deborah Watling-Poole. Aunt Dee, Miss Nancy.'

'Quite,' Miss Deborah Watling-Poole said, looking down through her tiny lorgnette at Nancy. 'A pleasure to meet you, Miss Nancy.'

'I'm sure,' Nancy said, taking the limply proffered hand. 'And you, Miss Watling-Poole.'

'Well, shall we go?' Lord Bryce said, rubbing his hands together.

'We shall arrive in quite sufficient time,' Miss Deborah said, transferring her gaze to her nephew. '*Idomeneo* is not one of Mozart's more important works.' She shifted her gaze to Nancy. 'Don't you agree, Miss Nancy?'

'I've never seen it,' Nancy admitted.

'Not very surprising. This is the first time it is being performed in London, and it is quite a hundred years old. Mozart died in 1791. He was an

Austrian. Have you read the score?'

'No,' Nancy said.

'Neither have I. I shouldn't be surprised. Not surprised at all.' With a satisfied shake of her head, Miss Deborah Watling-Poole advanced toward the door.

Nancy tried to sort that out, and then decided not to bother. She could see why Cousin Clothile had decided to come down with an unspecified disease. Taking her cape from Meb, she buttoned the collar and followed the wake of the advancing battleship.

In the coach, Aunt Dee gave a lecture on Discourtesy and Lack of Manners Among Americans I Have Known, which gradually turned into Lack of Moral Fibre Is Caused by Not Wearing Corsets, and thence to Debauchery Amongst the Working Classes. Her words came in long bursts, which were not always connected to the previous thought, with just little enough space between so that nobody else could say a word. Nancy, who was wearing a corset, had not had the opportunity to be discourteous, and could hardly be considered working class, failed to understand why each of Aunt Dee's points was punctuated by a sharp glance at her.

When the coach pulled up at Covent Garden, Miss Watling-Poole stopped abruptly in mid-sentence, glared one last time at Nancy, and emerged. Clearly carriage rides were for conversation, while entering the Opera House was for looking superior and marching toward one's box. Nancy and Lord Bryce followed as best they could, Lord Bryce waving the tickets in the air so that the ticket-taker wouldn't even attempt to slow down the imperious Watling-Poole.

When they attained their box, the next phase started. 'We are early!' Miss Watling-Poole stated, making it clear that this undesirable condition was none of her doing. 'Percy, do run down and purchase me a copy of the libretto.'

'Right-oh, Aunt Dee,' Lord Bryce said, leaving hat and cane on his seat as he retreated from the box.

The houselights were dimming when he returned, carrying the red-covered copy of the libretto. Aunt Dee stared her disapproval, and then moved to a seat in the rear of the box so she could read by the corridor-light by simply moving the curtain slightly aside. Nancy wondered what she was going to do if she caught the orchestra or the singers in a mistake. The most likely thing seemed to be an immediate general denunciation. Miss Watling-Poole would rise from her seat, stride to the front of the box, point a rigid finger of accusation at the offending party, and announce in stentorian tones the enormity of the crime — obviously due to the offender's being a working-class American who was not wearing a corset.

The music started, the curtain parted and the stage lights went up. Nancy was almost immediately caught up by the magic of the experience. The costumes were bright and colorful, the sets were extravagant, and everything seemed larger than life. When the music was cheerful, it buoyed the whole audience; and when it was sad, it saddened everyone. The fact that the actors were singing in German, and consequently Nancy soon had no idea whatsoever of what was going on, made little difference. What the man in the blue tights was accusing the man in the striped pantaloons of was immaterial when he did it with such magnificent melodic authority; and what the woman with the twenty petticoats was pleading for was unimportant when she achieved such eloquent vibrato. Nancy enjoyed every minute of it.

Lord Bryce had moved his chair over to the far corner of the box and was staring in silent befuddlement at the stage, except for occasional surreptitious glances at Nancy and Aunt Dee. Both hands were wrapped around his cane, which he kept twisting nervously. Nancy noted this without thinking about it, until in the middle of the second act his secret was revealed. A spotlight on the far side of the box came on to illuminate a group of conspirators who were loudly singing their secrets on stage left. The light glinted off the brass rail which went around the front of the box. And in that brass rail, as in a distorting mirror, Nancy could see a grotesque reflection of Lord Bryce.

After glancing around to be sure he wasn't being watched, which motion attracted Nancy's attention to the reflection in the brass rail, Lord Bryce slid a long glass tube from the top of his cane and tilted it to his lips.

Keeping her head turned away from Lord Bryce, Nancy smiled. She wondered whether he was a compulsive secret tippler, if he thought it was smart, or if he was escaping Aunt Dee's disapproval. She recalled that once Robert had come home from Harvard very angry after having purchased a similar cane, which was broken on the same day by a fellow student who twisted the handle off after Robert refused to divulge the secret of its opening.

Miss Watling-Poole didn't open her mouth through the whole opera. She did, however, occasionally tap the libretto sharply with her fingernail while shaking her head sadly. While Nancy was conscious of all of this byplay, she did not allow it to interfere with her enjoyment of the opera.

At the finish of the opera, when the

final curtain was pulled aside once more and the cast came back to life to take their bows, Nancy stood up and applauded vigorously. Lord Bryce joined in, but there was a subtle cast to his features, combined with the empty glass tube in his cane, that suggested to Nancy that he would have applauded a public execution, an active volcano, or a waterspout just as enthusiastically at that moment. Miss Watling-Poole touched the tips of her fingers together several times after drawing her gloves on. Nancy was unsure whether this represented applause or impatience.

They left by the side box stairs to escape the common herd of orchestra-seat holders, and stood by the side door waiting for their carriage to take its turn in pulling up and removing them from the vicinity of Covent Garden, which aside from the theater was considered an unsavory area to be in at night. People who looked to be of a decidedly lower caste than even Miss Watling-Poole's working class had gathered across the street to watch their betters leaving their evening's entertainment.

'Good show, what?' Lord Bryce suddenly said. 'What?' he insisted.

'Mozart has done better,' Aunt Dee announced, personally offended at the master's inadequacy. 'Better.'

'I enjoyed the opera very much,' Nancy told him. 'I am very glad I came.' She realized that it was true, and for almost three hours she had not thought about her problems, or the mysteries of Benjamin House.

'What!' Lord Bryce said firmly, waving his hollow cane in the air to attract the attention of his coachman, who had just driven around the corner in his turn.

'I am feeling indisposed,' Miss Watling-Poole announced as they settled in the coach. 'Take me home, Percy.'

'Of course,' Lord Bryce agreed. He thumped on the side of the coach, and then stuck his head out and yelled, 'Old Compton Street first, Stamford, and then Benjamin House!' Then he rolled up the window, leaned his head against the wall, and closed his eyes.

Miss Watling-Poole fought against her

indisposition by launching into an involved monologue about the opera, first-class travel by rail, shoes with heels, the detection of criminal types by the shape of their eyes, tatting and the road to salvation, oysters and sin; the whole path of this talk being intersected with numerous side roads, detours, and dead ends. Nancy stopped even pretending to be interested when she saw that Miss Watling-Poole was apparently speaking to a vast audience that existed in her own head.

Nancy thought that it would have been nice of Lord Bryce to warn her about his aunt. Perhaps he was afraid she wouldn't go. But he hadn't been paying any attention to her all evening, so what difference would it have made to him if she hadn't gone? What had been his motive in inviting Nancy along? A sudden impulse? Was he really attracted to her and just silenced by the awful presence of Aunt Dee?

They arrived at the Watling-Poole residence on Old Compton Street, and Lord Bryce excused himself to escort his aunt inside. After a minute he returned and, yelling a few cryptic words to the coachman, settled back inside. He seemed more awake now, more alert and sure of himself. 'I have been ignoring you,' he said, leaning forward and staring into Nancy's eyes.

'No you haven't,' Nancy protested.

'Yes I have. What did you think of the old lady?'

'Your aunt? She's, ah, very lively and strong-willed,' Nancy said, thinking it an odd question. He was still staring intently at her.

'She's insane, you know, quite insane,' he told her seriously. 'But one has one's familial obligations; and besides, she has a great deal of money.'

'Oh,' Nancy said lamely, completely at a loss for words.

'Your eyes sparkle,' Lord Bryce said. 'Would you like a drink?'

'A drink?' This young man was rapidly confusing her as much as his aunt had, although in an entirely different manner.

'Show you a little secret,' he said, picking up his cane and unscrewing the handle. 'My brandy-cane.' He removed a silver cup the size of a large thimble from atop the glass flask and poured it half-full of the amber liquid. 'A little libation, beautiful Miss Nancy? A toast to the gods — whichever ones are awake at the moment? We could sing it if you like.' And he proceeded to do so in a breaking tenor: 'To the gods whichever hear us. To Zeus and Hermes and Aph-ro-di-te. To the gods — to Mercury and what's-his-name, and Bacchus!'

'I don't think so, thank you.'

'You should be singing,' Lord Bryce complained. Then he paused to look sorrowful. 'You just think I'm being silly.'

'Not at all.'

His eyebrows arched. 'Not at *all?*'

'Well, perhaps a little.'

Lord Bryce gulped down his thimbleful and reassembled his cane. 'Of course I'm being silly,' he said morosely. 'I want to declare my undying love for you, and I'll just be laughed at.'

'Sir!' Nancy said, becoming alarmed.

'You see? Nancy, dear Nancy, why

must we wait for convention an' morality, when we know what we both want?'

Nancy's eyes grew wide. She couldn't sort out the meaning of what he'd just said, but the sense was clear. And he was getting noticeably drunker by the second. 'Please, Lord Bryce, just take me home,' she said calmly.

''At's where we're going, you know. Nancy, dear.' He put both hands to her head in what was supposed to be an affectionate gesture, but came closer to being a double blow. 'Nancy, you must call me Percy. My love.'

Nancy was willing to call him anything if he'd just keep his hands off her and stop breathing stale cognac in her face. 'Percy, this is so sudden,' she said, pushing his hands away. 'You must give me time to think about it.'

This was a mistake. He suddenly moved to the seat beside her and put his arms around her. 'Time!' he said. 'We know: you know, I know. Why must they know? Kiss me now, and I'll never tell. Just one little kiss, my darling.' His hug tightened.

'Let go!' Nancy screamed, now thoroughly frightened. But his grip was unbreakable for one of her strength, and her struggles only served to excite him more.

'Aha, you are a woman of spirit and passion,' Lord Bryce declared, pushing his face up against hers.

She turned away to escape his breath. 'Lord Bryce, you're intoxicated, and you're behaving disgracefully.'

He suddenly let go of her and slumped forward in his seat. 'You are less than enthusiastic,' he said, staring dolefully across at the front of the carriage.

Nancy repressed a tremendous urge to laugh. 'You are not behaving like a gentleman,' she told him, patting awkwardly at her hair to get it into some semblance of order.

Lord Bryce grabbed her hand with both of his and regarded her earnestly. 'Miss Hooker — Nancy — I find that I am tremendously fond of you. I might even say passionately. I cannot but find it hard to believe that you don't reciprocate this passion. We are unconventional people, Nancy. Should we bow down to convention when our whole lives is involved — are involved?'

'Lord Bryce . . . '

'Percy!'

'Percy. We hardly know each other. Don't you think we should get to know each other better before making such decisions?' Nancy tried to pick her words very carefully, so as to avoid either encouraging or angering the ardent Percy. 'You must certainly give me time to decide properly how I feel about you. And I don't somehow feel that the interior of a moving vehicle is the proper place for a declaration of affection.'

'I feel very strongly toward you,' Lord Bryce said. 'And I am a very impatient man. A man of action. You can tell I'm a man of action, can't you?'

'Yes, I assure you.'

'Right.' He nodded as though he had just established some very important point, and started caressing Nancy's hand as if it were a silver teapot he was polishing. 'And when I want something, I take it. Without waiting for a by-your-leave or a how's-your-fancy, I take it. When I want it. I'm a violent and passionate man, Nancy.'

Nancy didn't care much for Lord Bryce's version of courting, and was getting more and more nervous every moment. There was no telling what Lord Bryce might decide to do next. Nancy had no experience in dealing with a violent, passionate, amorous drunk. The safest course seemed to lie in keeping him talking until they arrived at Benjamin House. 'I can see that you're a very strong-willed person,' she said.

'Passionate!' he insisted, clasping her hand to his breast.

She wrenched the hand free. 'Please, Lord Bryce!' Nancy saw the situation as dangerous and, at the same time, ludicrous. Aside from a growing fear, combined incongruously with an impulse to laugh aloud at this bumbling man, Nancy felt developing within her a strong sense of resentment. Lord Bryce was ruining for her the memory of what had been a thrilling evening: her first London opera. If this had to happen, couldn't it have happened some other day?

Lord Bryce broke apart his cane again and, without bothering to use the silver cup as an intermediary, drained the rest of the contents of his flask. He tried to reassemble the cane, fumbling for a minute with the delicate threading, then threw the pieces onto the opposite seat in disgust. For a long minute he sat brooding in the corner, while Nancy maintained a careful silence. Then he turned to her, a crafty expression on his face. His eyes were focused somewhat past her face. 'I'm going to be quite a rich man, you know,' he told her. 'Quite 'pressively rich. In the not-too-distant future, I shall have money.' He waved a vague hand in the air. 'All sorts of money. Could do worse. We'll be friends, you and I.'

Watching him, Nancy had the not unreasonable hope that he would pass out any minute. The few men she had seen under the extreme influence of alcohol had quietly gone to sleep shortly after reaching the slurred language stage. But these had been older men, friends of her father, celebrating some important occasion like an election or a marriage. She wasn't sure of the effect on a younger, 'passionate' man like Lord Bryce. She wondered about this sudden talk of money, but didn't want to encourage him by asking questions. Better stick to some neutral subject, and keep him talking until he fell asleep or they arrived at Benjamin Hall. It surely couldn't be too long now. 'Did you enjoy the opera, Lord — Percy?'

'Opera?' Lord Bryce scoffed, rejecting the whole concept. 'Stage-acting. Can't compare to tragedy and drama of life. Da — dashed singing all the time.'

Here was a man, Nancy thought, who thought nothing of throwing himself at a lady in a carriage, but corrected himself before using a bad word. A true gentleman. There was something very sad about the thought, and about Lord Bryce.

'You're laughing at me!' Lord Bryce suddenly accused.

'No, honestly, I'm not,' Nancy said, realizing she must have smiled.

'You don't take me seriously. Nobody

takes me seriously. And I'm going to have a lot of money — be an important man. Then you'll take me seriously.'

'I'm sorry,' Nancy said. 'I didn't mean — '

'I am serious!' Lord Bryce shouted, throwing his arms around her and pinning her to the wall of the coach. 'You'll see, Nancy. Dear Nancy. You'll respect me. Kiss me, Nancy!' And he pressed his lips against her neck in a slobbering gesture of affection.

Nancy tried to push him away, but found herself being turned and forced beneath him on the leather seat as he twisted himself around on top of her. One part of her mind tried to stay calm, and find a sensible way out of this intolerable situation, but she suddenly realized that she was sobbing hysterically and beating her fists against his shoulders. Tears obscured her vision, and all she could feel was the pressure of his body on top of her and his wet lips trying to make contact with her mouth as she wildly shook her head from side to side.

He was yelling now, and she was

screaming, and he seemed to be growing more excited by the motion of her body under his. 'Hold still, damn it!' he finally shouted, grabbing her hands and pinning them above her head. He half-rose from the seat to thrust his body more directly on hers. She pulled her knees up beneath him as he did and then, when he came down, thrust upward with all her strength. He was thrown from her, to crash half on the floor and half on the opposite seat.

Nancy swung up and unlatched one of the carriage doors. Lord Bryce grabbed her around the waist as the door swung open, but she kicked backwards and he released her, causing her to be expelled from the carriage as from a slingshot. She saw the wheels of the carriage, and the cobblestones beneath her, and for a fleeting instant Lord Bryce staring down at her with a horrified expression on his face, his mouth open in a vast O. Then something slammed down on the back of her shoulders. A point of blackness expanded to engulf her, and there was complete silence.

* * *

Clop, clopclop, clop, clopclop. Nancy was resting quietly in her bed in the little room over her father's, and it wasn't quite time to get up and do the chores yet. The bed, or perhaps the whole room, was swaying delightfully from side to side, and she could hear the steady footsteps of her old horse coming upstairs to wake her. *Clop clop clop.* There was something wrong with that image, but she didn't care what, and drifted back to sleep to wait for the horse to arrive.

Clop, clopclop, clop. Clop, clopclop, clop. She was resting comfortably on a boat, being pulled by a horse. Of course — it must be the Erie Barge Canal, and they were finally taking that trip her father had promised her. Why couldn't she remember getting on? No matter; she went back to sleep.

Clop, clopclop, clop. Clop, clopclop, clop. Her head pounded, and she couldn't figure out why. She opened her eyes, and for a time could focus on nothing. Blobs of light kept moving into

187

her view and then past. When she started to focus, she could see they were streetlights, but then her eyes hurt as badly as her head and she closed them. Something had happened. What? She couldn't remember. And where was she? She had no idea. She almost went back to sleep, but the steady motion beat against the rhythm of the throbbing in her head, and was slowly and painfully waking her up. The steady motion of what? She lay still and tried to think about it.

She was in a trap of some kind, being driven somewhere; she could hear the steady hoof-beats of the horse on the road. She was lying down; that explained the streetlights passing in front of her. Streetlights? She was in a city. Boston?

London!

Memory came flooding back to her, and she knew what had happened. She must have been knocked unconscious when she fell from the carriage. But this wasn't the same carriage. What could have happened since then? She looked around her. She was indeed lying supine in the back of some sort of trap. She could make out the driver's back as he hunched over the seat. The gaslights popped into view over his shoulder and then floated along until they were out of view behind her like a steady string of illuminated bubbles.

Nancy tried to sit up and a sharp pain lanced into her shoulder, causing her to drop back down with an audible groan.

The driver looked around. 'You're awake, mum,' he said unnecessarily. 'How are you feeling?'

William! It was Alan DeWit's servant who was smiling — or leering — down at her. She groaned again and closed her eyes. After a second she peered through one half-closed lid to see that William had resumed driving. He would think she had fallen back into unconsciousness, as indeed she would have had not the realization of the identity of her driver snapped through the throbbing pain to bring her fully awake.

She must carefully get up and over the side of the trap before William realized she was awake. She must be gone before he knew she was going. She forced herself to think of what each part of her body must do as she rolled over and pushed herself up to a sitting position. The world whirled around her and she almost fell back down, but she clutched the sides of the trap and painfully held herself up. Now she must roll off the side of the trap and onto the street without making a sound. No — she must roll off the back or she would fall under the wheel. She must do it now, before William looked back and saw her, or before he arrived at wherever he was abducting her to. For some reason she pictured a vast underground cave, with William pulling her ever deeper and deeper into its unknown depths.

She gathered her legs under her and leaned against the back board. Then she fell sideways, and the pain in her arm came to a sharp peak, feeling like a living thing trying to rip its way out. She froze in that position, with her teeth clamped tight against an inadvertent cry, willing William not to turn around. After a few seconds, when he hadn't, she slowly righted herself again.

The clopping horse was slowly pulled to a stop, and William turned around. He quickly jumped down from his seat when he saw her crouched in the corner. 'Be careful, mum,' he said. 'You'll hurt yourself.' He reached out to hold her, his big hands going gently around her back. 'We're home now. I'll help you inside.'

Nancy looked up and saw the twin-towered front of Benjamin House looming before her. Then all was black again.

10

It was day when Nancy woke; the curtains were drawn full back and sunlight washed the room. Prudence was sitting in a straight-backed chair by the bed, stitching the hem of a dress. When she saw that Nancy's eyes were open, she leaned over and put her hand on her forehead. 'How do you feel, child?' she asked.

'I'm all right,' Nancy said, cautiously moving her body to make sure it was true. 'My shoulder hurts, but that seems to be the only damage. How long have I been sleeping?'

'It's about noon, or shortly after,' Prudence told her. 'You gave us all a bad fright last night, what with William carrying you in like a sack of potatoes. What happened?'

Such a glamorous image, Nancy thought. 'Didn't William tell you?' (Yes, what did William say? What was he doing there?)

'Apparently William happened by as you leapt from Lord Bryce's carriage. The young gentleman was too' — sniff — 'intoxicated to render assistance himself, so William brought you home.'

'Lord Bryce was filthy drunk,' Nancy said. 'He attempted to make improper advances toward me — ' (*How stilted and dry the words make it sound,* Nancy thought as she remembered Lord Bryce clutching at her and slobbering in her ear.) ' — so I elected to leave his carriage.' She smiled. 'Unfortunately it was still in motion at the time, so I didn't leave too steadily.'

'That is the image that emerged from William's story,' Prudence said. 'It was very fortunate that he happened along. Robert has been trying to locate Lord Bryce all morning, but that noble young gentleman seems to have gone out of town. I'll bring you some tea.' She put aside the dress she had been hemming and stalked from the room.

Is no one but me, Nancy wondered, *going to think it odd that William happened to be there at exactly that time?*

He must have been following me. I admit it was irrational to think he was dragging me off to some secret hideaway — the sort of thing Gayle would think of. Only she'd think it was romantic! It's a lucky thing he was following me, whatever his intentions were. I wonder what he'd think if I were to thank him for doing so. I suppose I should thank him for rescuing me, in any case.

Prudence returned with the tea; and Robert, Alan DeWit and Dr. Moran followed in her wake. 'Glad you're all right,' Robert said soberly. 'We seem to be developing a proclivity for being bumped about, don't we?'

Nancy took his hand. 'Let us hope it's not setting a precedent,' she said, smiling.

'When I get ahold of that — gentleman — I shall do some bashing of my own!' Robert said in a voice devoid of emotion.

'Please, Robert,' Nancy said. 'He was drunk, and it's over and done with now. I'd just as soon forget about it.'

'He was a swine, and I could kick myself for letting you go out with him. Hell of a brother I am. Excuse me.'

'How could you know?' Nancy asked. '*I* didn't know, and a woman's intuition is supposed to warn her of things like that.'

Dr. Moran stepped forward. 'How does your shoulder feel?' he asked briskly.

'Stiff,' Nancy told him.

'Nothing broken,' he stated. 'Just banged up and bruised, to put it in layman's terms. Bandaged it up last night. Wear one of those leg-o'-mutton sleeves, and no one will know. Fine in a week. Blame myself, you know. I introduced him to you. Never forgive myself. Never suspected. Always a perfect gentleman around me.'

Nancy smiled, trying to picture Lord Bryce making a passionate advance toward Dr. Moran. 'He would be, Doctor,' she assured him. 'It's not your fault. How could you know?'

Alan was sitting on a chair across the room, staring morosely at the bed. Nancy couldn't decide what he was thinking. 'Mister DeWit,' she said, 'thank your man William for me, will you? I shall thank him myself when I see him. It was very lucky that he was there just at that moment.'

'Yes,' Alan said. 'I thought so myself. I'm glad — I — that is — Do take care of yourself, Miss Nancy.' There was an undercurrent of some powerful emotion in his voice that seemed to be making him inarticulate.

Nancy sipped at her tea. 'Is there any reason I should remain in bed, Doctor Moran?' she asked.

'Not if you feel like rising,' he assured her. 'Don't play any cricket today.'

'I'll restrain myself. Now, if you'll all excuse me, I'd like to get dressed.'

Mumbling various cheery things, they all left the room, and Nancy pushed the blanket aside and swung her feet onto the floor. She found that she had to favor the injured shoulder, and that lesser aches and pains appeared throughout her body; but she felt very well considering all she'd been through. The wide sleeves of her shirtwaist did, as Dr. Moran had said, cover the bandages and hide them completely. There was a stiffness in her hip that made her walk a bit oddly, but it wasn't serious. *I look like a perfectly normal, healthy woman with a funny walk,* she decided, practicing in front of the mirror.

As she was finishing dressing, Meb knocked on the door. 'Lady Gayle has arrived to see you, mum,' she said.

'How nice. Please ask her to come up.'

'Dreadful, absolutely dreadful!' Gayle declaimed as she entered the room. 'You're not in bed? I thought you were ruined, or at least grievously injured.'

'I'm sorry to be such a disappointment, Gayle. I will try to do better next time.'

'You're walking funny,' Gayle said. 'You have a broken leg, which you're making every effort to conceal so as not to have your family find out.'

'Who told you?'

'Your brother, Lord Benjamin. Robert.'

'Darn!' Nancy said. 'And I was so hoping he wouldn't find out.'

'Nancy, there is no romance in your entire body.'

'None,' Nancy agreed. 'Just various pains and bruises and . . . Gayle!'

'What is it?' Gayle asked, looking startled.

'Your dress — I forgot all about it. Your beautiful dress. It must have been ruined.' She looked around the room. 'I don't know . . . Oh there it is, over the chair.'

Gayle picked it up and they both examined it. It was ripped in the shoulder, scraped and mud-splattered. 'I shall hang it in a prominent place in my room,' Gayle declared. 'And when anyone asks, I shall have a tale of heroic love and romance to explain its tattered condition. You won't mind if I mention your name?'

'I shall most assuredly mind if you mention my name,' Nancy told her.

'Now, Nancy, you must tell me all about it,' Gayle said, sitting back comfortably in the chair. 'Remember that I didn't like that creature from the first.'

'But you advised me to go to the opera with him,' Nancy reminded her.

'Of course. Dear Nancy, I didn't think he was going to attack you. What happened?'

'When we left the opera,' Nancy said in a low voice, 'he made a strange gesture with his hand. At that moment, five lascars, who had been hiding in the shadows, leaped out and grabbed me.'

'Yes?' Gayle said, her eyes wide.

'They stuffed me in a sack and tied the top. The next thing I knew, I was on board a Chinese junk, heading out to sea. I was surrounded by evil-looking men with funny beards.'

'What happened?' Gayle demanded.

Nancy shrugged. 'I disappeared and was never seen or heard from again.'

'Nancy, you're pulling my leg.'

'It's true, Gayle. But you really don't want to hear about it. It was dull and nasty and not in the slightest romantic or adventurous. All I felt was frightened and disgusted.'

'An adventure is never an adventure to the person it happens to,' Lady Gayle explained patiently. 'It's only an adventure to the people she tells about it afterward. Surely you can see that. Think of all the famous adventures and romances you've ever read, and tell me if you'd like any of them to actually happen to you.'

'I'd just as soon this one had never happened,' Nancy told Gayle. 'Come, let's walk around somewhere. I feel the exercise would be very good for me.'

They walked downstairs and through the study and library, and out onto the grounds in the rear of the house. 'A formal garden,' Gayle said, sounding pleased as she looked over the carefully mowed lawn and trimmed hedges. 'How nice.' She went over to examine the closest clump of flowers. 'Azaleas and brush-bottoms and dahlias. And what are these pink and blue ones — the ones with the cupped leaves?'

'I have no idea,' Nancy said. 'Ask me about corn, or squash, or string beans, and I can tell you sire and dam; but the only thing I know about flowers are tulips, and none of these are tulips.'

'Deckle,' a voice said. It had the sound of gravel going down a chute. Now that he had spoken, the owner of the voice became visible. He was standing beside a tree: a small man, gnarled and wrinkled and discolored like the ancient wood, holding a spade as high as he was, so still that he might have taken root any time in the past ten years. He wasn't looking at the women, but off to the side, as if as long as he could see them in the corner of his vision it wasn't worth the trouble of moving his head to see them straight on.

'Excuse me?' Nancy said, staring at the strange man.

'Deckle,' he repeated. 'Them's yon flower with the pink and blue blossoms. Deckle. Put 'em in meself, I did, back in sixty-six. No — sixty-seven, year of the fire.'

'Fire?' Gayle asked.

'Yes'm. Done pretty well since then, they has. Heard you mention tulips, mum. They won't grow here worth nothin'.'

'What fire?' Gayle persisted.

The man shifted his gaze to look at her without moving so much as his head. 'Couple years before them tennymen houses were put in up by the break. Were a break before them houses. Fine stand of trees cut down to put them houses in. Lumber stacked to dry. Good wood. Whole stack burned out. Most took the house with it. Fire.'

'You must be the gardener,' Nancy said.

'Must,' he agreed. 'Name's Burton.' He nodded with some secret satisfaction. 'Old Burton.'

'I'm Miss Nancy,' Nancy said. 'My brother's Lord Benjamin. Robert. I'm sorry I didn't meet you with the others.'

'Reckened you were, mum.' He touched his forehead. 'Them's inside you met; I'm outside. Me and my son. Seth, his name is, but they always calls him Young Burton. Pleased.' He touched his forehead again.

'And I'm pleased to meet you,' Nancy told him. 'You've done a beautiful job here.'

Burton nodded. 'Try to keep it up. Thank you, miss.' He shifted the spade to his other hand. 'Got to spile the gabbage.' And with a final salute, he was off down the hedgerow.

Nancy looked at Gayle. 'Did he really say he was going to 'spile the gabbage'?'

'That's what I heard,' Gayle agreed.

'I thought I spoke the language.'

'Don't look at me. I was laboring under the same belief, and I was born here.'

'Let's find out,' Nancy said, leading the way back into the library, where she remembered seeing a large dictionary. 'Spile,' she said meditatively, flipping the pages of the dictionary. 'Spile. Here we are. Spile: a small plug, used to stop a vent. Also: a large stake driven into the ground as a support for some superstructure.'

'Fine,' Gayle said. 'Now just discover whether a gabbage is a vent or a superstructure, and we'll have it solved.'

'Nary a gabbage,' Nancy said after further inspection of the massive book. 'Could he have said gabbard?'

'He could have said anything. I only know I heard 'gabbage.''

'A gabbard is a lighter, or barge, or similar vessel. It's an obsolete Scots word.'

'Fine,' Gayle said. 'He's either plugging up a lighter, or driving stakes into a barge. If he is Scottish, which he isn't. I suppose we could sneak out and see what he's doing.'

'No, thank you,' Nancy said. 'If there's a barge in my garden, I'd just as soon not know about it.'

'As you say,' Gale agreed, picking up a book at random and leafing through it. 'No pictures or conversations,' she announced, putting the book down. 'And what's the use of a book without pictures or conversations?'

''Ware of white rabbits,' Nancy said. 'Here's something that should interest you, as you like adventures and romances.' She went to the shelf where she had replaced *The Benjamin Legend*, and retrieved it.

Gayle leafed through the pages slowly. 'Now here is romance,' she said. '*I* don't have a legend.'

'I'm sure that before you're too much older, you will have.'

Gayle looked at her sharply, but then went back to the book. 'It's in the cellar,' she said. 'He says the treasure's in the cellar.'

'No,' Nancy corrected. 'He says it *isn't* in the cellar. He says it isn't anywhere, but most especially not in the cellar.'

Gayle looked up, wrinkling her nose. 'Of course, what would you expect him to say? And that means it must be in the cellar. Have you looked?'

'No. And even if there were a treasure, and it were in the cellar, do you think we could find it after people have spent two hundred years looking for it?'

'I expect we could certainly try!'

'Gayle!' Nancy said, putting her hand to her mouth. 'I had forgotten. Somebody made a map — I found it in the book. Wait a minute; you stay here and read the book and I'll get it from my room.' Nancy fairly ran upstairs, until her sprained hip forcibly reminded her of its existence, and then she proceeded with more leisured haste until she had returned with the document.

'What is it?' Gayle asked, examining it closely. 'I can't make heads or tails of it. It doesn't resemble any map I've ever seen.'

'Look here,' Nancy said, flipping through the book until she came to the page. 'See how it corresponds to this old drawing of the cellar? Here, hold it this way.'

'Ah, quite. Yes. That's what it is, indeed. But there doesn't seem to be any line or set of directions to follow. No X marks the spot, or dig here, or any such. Just a few extra squiggles round and about. What do you think it means?'

'It means someone else thought the treasure is down in the cellar — and quite recently, too. Of course they didn't know just where the treasure was, or they would have just taken it, wouldn't they?'

'Perhaps they did,' Gayle said darkly. 'They wouldn't tell you about it, you know. Rightful owner and all that. What do you mean, quite recently?'

Nancy told Gayle of her deductions concerning the map. Without planning to, she continued, telling Gayle of the things that had happened to her since her arrival at Benjamin House, and her suspicions and fears.

'Well!' Gayle said finally, staring at her. 'For a person who doesn't believe in romance, you lead the strangest life. So that's why you were so curious about Alan DeWit, is it? And you think William was following us in the wax museum? And William must have been following you while you were out with Lord Bryce! They're afraid you'll discover something;

find out part of the secret before they've made off with the treasure themselves. It *must* be the treasure. Lord Alan must need the money to pay off some gambling debts. They are debts of honor, you know, and he'd have to shoot himself if he failed to pay them,' Gayle stated positively.

'Shoot himself?' Nancy asked.

'It happens all the time,' Gayle assured her.

'I think fact and fancy are irretrievably mixed in your head. Even if you were right about the rest of it, why should they follow me around to make sure I don't discover whatever there is to discover? What could I possibly find out in a wax museum, or at an opera?'

'Ah! But how could they know you were going to the wax museum — or be sure you were going to the opera? They have to keep watch on you at all times. Part of the secret must lie outside this house. Now that you've told me, they will have to start following me around too.'

'Gayle,' Nancy said, 'how could they possibly know that I've told you?'

Gayle's voice dropped to a conspiratorial whisper. 'They may be listening right at this very moment!' she insisted. 'Besides, they'll know soon enough after we explore the cellar.'

'And when are we going to explore the cellar?'

'Right now,' Gayle said. 'Unless you're frightened.'

'If I thought you were right, I should be scared to death. But even though I suspect Alan DeWit of attempting to kill my brother, and of following me around — or having his man follow me — I cannot believe that we're just going to stumble over a two-hundred-and-fifty-year-old treasure in the cellar.'

'Then why is he doing it?'

'I only wish I could figure that out.'

'Then it's settled,' Gayle said firmly. 'On to the cellar! Where are the stairs?'

'I don't know.'

'Fine help you are. I know — the map!' Gayle went back to examining it. 'Here — this must be it. This thing that looks like a stairway. See it? Now where would that come out up here?'

'I have no idea,' Nancy said.

'We'll just have to find out.'

'Why don't I ask one of the servants?'

Gayle shook her head, her nose wrinkled with scorn. 'How do we know they're not in league with Alan? Besides, we should certainly be able to find a simple staircase by ourselves. If we can't do that, how could we ever hope to locate the treasure?' She stared at the map for a minute, mumbling to herself. Then she folded it and tucked it into her blouse. 'Somewhere by the kitchen or the butler's pantry. We will need candles, or a lantern.'

'The butler's pantry!' Nancy said. 'I heard strange noises coming from under the floor.'

'Candles,' Gayle repeated.

They retreated down the corridor and into the dining room. Gayle listened dramatically for a moment at the door to the butler's pantry, and then nodded and they went in. Nancy was beginning to feel like a conspirator. 'Listen,' she said, 'it's my house. Why shouldn't we go down to the cellar if we feel like it?'

'Hush!' Gayle said, her ear to the kitchen door. 'There are people in there. They'll hear you.'

'Oh, never mind. We'll do it your way. Here are a couple of glass-chimney lanterns. Wait a moment.' She twisted a spill from a piece of newspaper and lit one of the lanterns. Then they looked around for a stairway door, but with no success.

'The kitchen?' Nancy suggested.

'A last resort,' Gayle replied. 'We should have to wait until it was empty. I know!' She ran around, through the dining room and out into the corridor. 'One of these doors here. I should have thought of it.'

Nancy followed her, feeling foolish with the lantern in her hand. But then, when she opened the first door and found a stairway leading down, the feeling of foolishness evaporated. Despite her misgivings, she found that her heart was beating faster as they went down the narrow stairs. What would they find down there? Was it possible that the Benjamin treasure had lain below for all these many years?

Whatever Nancy expected when she started down the stairway, it wasn't what she found. The cellar was a rabbit warren of stone-walled passages, with heavy beams holding up the board ceiling. The doors to the rooms were ancient and massive, with great wrought-iron hinges and bolts. The first was a vegetable-room, and the second contained bins of coal and coke, with a metal slide going up to a trap in the ceiling. The third was piled full of wood for the fireplaces.

Nancy found that she was shivering as they went from room to room. 'I should have brought a shawl,' she said. 'It's cold and dank, and very commonplace. So much for romance.'

'We have just begun,' Gayle informed her. 'Look, this room is locked. I wonder what's in here?'

Nancy saw that there was a large padlock on the next door. 'That's odd,' she said. 'I wonder what anyone would want to keep locked up down here.'

Both women froze as they heard the steady tramp of footsteps coming down the staircase. 'Put out the light!' Gayle whispered.

'Too late,' Nancy whispered back, feeling prickles on the back of her neck. 'Whoever it is, he must have seen it by now. Look!' And she pointed to where the glow of a second lantern was weaving and bobbing about in time with the footsteps.

First the feet appeared, shod in proper black shoes; then dark trousers, then a jacket and a vest, and finally a face.

'Fenton!' Nancy gasped.

'Miss Nancy,' Fenton said calmly, coming down the last steps and advancing toward them.

'What are you doing here?' Nancy asked before she had time to think about it.

'I am going to the larder. Cook has asked me to obtain certain items for dinner. May I assist you?'

A polite way to turn the question around. 'We're just exploring,' Gayle said.

'Indeed?'

'Mushrooms!' Nancy burst out. 'I'm looking for a place to grow mushrooms.'

Fenton nodded, as though nothing she

could do would surprise him, and turned to go down a side-passage.

'Fenton!' Nancy called. 'Before you go, could you tell me what's in here?'

'Ah, yes.' Fenton turned back. 'That is a box-room. Luggage and the like.' He extracted a key from his ring and came over to the door. 'Always keep it locked,' he said, unfastening the huge padlock. 'I don't really remember why, miss. Habit, I suppose. Hasn't been opened in years.' He put his shoulder to the door, and it slowly creaked open. 'If that will be all, miss? If you'd just close it behind you; no point in locking it now.' He gave a stiff bow and marched down the passage.

The room was full of boxes: trunk piled upon trunk and valise stacked upon valise. None of them were new, and some looked quite old indeed. They ranged from incredibly beat-up to scarcely ever used. 'I wonder what's in them,' Nancy said.

Gayle was obviously swayed by curiosity, but she resisted. 'That's for another day,' she said firmly. 'Obviously what we're looking for isn't in here.'

213

'How can you be sure? Have you never heard of the purloined letter? Hidden in the most obvious place.'

'If we don't find the treasure anywhere else, we'll go through here trunk by trunk.'

They returned to the passage, faithfully closing the door behind them. Fenton's footsteps heralded his return. 'Miss Nancy,' he said, 'I don't profess any knowledge of the horticulture of fungi, but you might find the climate you are seeking down in the second basement.'

'Second basement?' Nancy echoed.

'Yes, miss. Down this corridor and to the left you will find a stairway. It leads to the second basement. If I might venture to say so, miss, you might need a wrap: it is quite chill and damp down there.' With another half-bow, he clumped up the stairs.

'How wonderful!' Gayle said. 'Let's go!'

'What about that wrap?' Nancy asked, rubbing her arms. 'There's quite enough chill and damp here.'

'Next time,' Gayle said. 'Oh do come on. We'll only go down there for a few minutes.'

The stairs were of rough-cut stone, and they turned a sharp corner without bothering to pause for a landing. The lower half widened out like a cornucopia, spilling into a large stone chamber. The lamp flickered as they entered, tugged at by some unknown breeze, and for a breathless moment it threatened to go out. Its solitary brightness was insufficient to illuminate this great room; it did no more than cast grotesque shadows about the walls, which served to heighten the sense of gloom that pervaded the underground chamber. But had it gone out, both women realized, gloom would then change to fear and terror in the darkness. The upper cellar was merely a natural part of the great house, but this was alien and strange, and promised dark purposes and unnatural secrets.

'Where do you suppose the breeze is coming from?' Gayle whispered.

'Let us look around,' Nancy said, speaking in a normal voice to help dispel the eerie feeling that had gripped them both.

Look around . . . around . . . the room

threw back at her in a mocking echo that was slow to die.

'Nancy!' Gayle said, clutching her free hand. And again the echo: *Nancy . . . Nancy . . . ancy . . . ancy.*

'It's only an echo,' Nancy said, speaking calmly, although she could feel her heart pounding in her chest.

Echo . . . echo . . . echo, the great chamber confirmed.

'I don't like echoes!' Gayle whispered.

'I understand,' Nancy replied in a low voice. 'I admit to a growing lack of fondness for them myself. Come on.'

'You either really have no imagination,' Gayle said, her hands digging into Nancy's arm, 'or you're very brave.'

'I have more imagination than I like at this moment,' Nancy said, watching the shadows dart about the walls as the lamp flickered, 'but I will not be frightened away by an echo.' *Frightened, yes,* she added to herself, *but not frightened away.*

'Stay close to me!' Gayle said as Nancy advanced slowly into the room.

'Don't worry,' Nancy whispered back. 'I won't go anywhere without you. I never dreamed there was anything like this under Benjamin House.'

Gayle had no need to ask what the 'like this' referred to. They slowly walked out onto a floor of great uneven stones, worn smooth by the passage of time and the feet of whoever had used this room, for whatever purpose.

'Watch it!' Gayle said, tugging Nancy to a stop.

Watch it . . . it . . . it . . . it, the room repeated. Gayle drew even closer to Nancy and pointed down. There, almost at her feet, yawned a great circular pit, some twelve feet in diameter. Nancy repressed a shudder and held the lantern out. The walls of the pit were faced with brick, going down about four feet before meeting a stone floor. There was a thick wooden post set into the center of the pit. It was about six feet high, and had some rusted and decaying objects fastened to it at various heights.

'What on Earth was that for?' Gayle whispered.

'I'd rather not speculate,' Nancy said.

'Your ancestors had a rather macabre

217

taste in cellars,' Gayle said. 'Look, over here. The source of the draught.' Set into the wall to their right was a wide stone fireplace, which quickly narrowed to a funnel-like top that disappeared into the wall.

'Well,' Nancy said, 'I wish we could get it lit. It would dispel some of the chill.'

'And the dark,' Gayle said. 'There's wood by the side here.'

Nancy inspected the stack of logs set into another niche in the stone wall. 'I wonder how long they've been sitting there,' she said. 'There's no kindling.'

'That's true,' Gayle said, looking around. 'Nancy! We could use the lamp!'

'What? Oh, of course, the kerosene. But the lamp will go out.'

'Not if we pour some out and then screw the base back on before the wick has a chance to dry out.'

'It's worth a try,' Nancy said. 'But we'd better be very careful.'

Nancy set the lantern down, and the two women struggled to get a couple of the hefty logs into the fireplace. When they had them in good position, Nancy retrieved the lantern and carefully unscrewed the base. While she held the upper part, Gayle sloshed kerosene over the logs. Then Nancy screwed the base back on. 'That part's done,' she said. 'Success. Now to get it lit.'

After some searching, they found a suitable stick in the log-crypt. Nancy held it down the chimney of the lantern until the end was burning firmly; then she thrust it at the logs. Nothing happened, so she moved the stick from place to place, trying to get the log to catch.

Suddenly, with a whooshing sound, a sheet of flame covered the fireplace, the sudden blast of heat causing Nancy to drop the stick and step backward as she felt it on her face. 'I think you were over-generous with the kerosene,' she said.

After a minute the flame died down. Part of the bark on the outer log had caught, and was sending up its own red-blue flame with a contented popping sound.

The women continued their exploration of the stone chamber. The fire gave them little additional light to see by, but they could look back at it and gain a sense of comfort from its presence. The other side of the chamber held a series of small rooms, each with a heavy wooden door with a small barred window. Most of the doors were now ajar, frozen in place by their rusty lunges.

'This must have been a prison,' Gayle whispered. 'An underground dungeon. These are certainly cells.'

'I was rather hoping they were for storing potatoes,' Nancy whispered back. They looked inside one and saw that the rear half was covered with a thick layer of black mud.

'What do you suppose . . . ?' Gayle asked.

'Straw, for bedding,' Nancy whispered. 'That's what it was two hundred years ago.'

'Not big on sanitary facilities, were they? I don't think the Prison Reform Commission would approve.'

Nancy pictured a group of elderly gentlemen with top hats and side whiskers going from cell to cell, peering about and making disapproving remarks in their notebooks.

Further along, toward the back of the room, was a large portal with a gate made of thick wrought-iron bars. It was the entrance to some sort of hall or corridor that extended from the chamber. Nancy and Gayle peered through the bars, holding their lantern aloft, but the light died out before showing anything but rough stone walls and a hard-packed earthen floor. The gate was locked, with a large padlock thrust through two iron rings that held a bolt securely in a hole in the stone wall.

'That's funny,' Gayle said. 'Look — the padlock isn't rusted.'

Nancy touched it and rubbed her fingers together. 'It's been oiled,' she said. She held the lantern up and examined the great hinges. 'These have been oiled too. Someone must be using this gate. I wonder what lies beyond it?'

'I wonder . . .' Gayle echoed. She reached into her blouse and pulled out the map. 'Nancy, set the lantern down, and let's see if we can make anything out of this.'

Nancy did so and they examined the map together. It took them a while to make sense of the drawing, but after Gayle figured out that the two layers of the cellar had been drawn side by side, they began to see the pattern.

'Here's this room,' Gayle said, touching the map with her finger.

'That's right,' Nancy agreed. 'There are the stairs. And those are the cells along the wall.'

'And this corridor goes off and makes a right turn. And there are some larger rooms off it up there. And it sort of dies out.'

Nancy peered at it for a while. 'Now why would anyone cut an extra thirty feet of corridor this far underground, if it doesn't go anywhere?'

'On the map it doesn't,' Gayle said excitedly. 'We'll have to get in there and look.'

'We'll have to find out who has the key first. And I'll bet it isn't Fenton.'

'We could break the padlock off,' Gayle suggested.

'We'd need a stout iron bar, and

someone a lot stronger than either you or I.'

'Then we will recruit. Perhaps through an advertisement in the paper.'

'I'm starting to shiver,' Nancy said. 'I rather think it's about time to leave.'

'This time I'll agree with you,' Gayle said, standing up and folding and putting away the map. 'Nancy — look at that! What do you make of it? No, stand up and leave the lantern on the ground. See there!'

Nancy looked where Gayle was pointing. 'Just the floor,' she said. She put her head closer to the bars. 'Oh, I see what you mean. Some of the earth's a different color from the rest. Gayle, that's freshly dug earth. It must have spilled from a wheelbarrow or something. Someone's been digging in there!'

A gust of wind tugged at her skirt, and a sudden popping from the logs in the fireplace sounded like distant laughter.

'Let's get out of here,' Gayle whispered.

Holding hands, they went back to the staircase. Their footsteps echoed and re-echoed through the stone chamber.

11

Robert had resolved to come down to dinner, and Nancy had resolved to tell him her suspicions. While she was dressing, she tried to decide just what it was that she could tell him. That someone had pushed that stone off the ledge? That William was following her around? That someone — perhaps the same mysterious someone — had been digging in the cellar? It could too easily sound foolish, but she would have to make it sound real. She needed Robert; there was no one else she could trust for help and advice.

When she came down to dinner, she found that Robert had asked Dr. Moran to join them, and after dinner the good doctor showed no inclination to leave. Not that he, or anybody but Nancy, knew of any reason why he should. Any other evening she would have been delighted to listen to his stories, but tonight she wanted to have a private talk with her brother, and Dr. Moran's presence made that impossible.

'We are living in an age when everything is on the verge of being known,' he said, warming his hands on his cup of coffee, having turned down the brandy that Robert was drinking. 'As someone has said, it is merely a matter of filling in the final decimal places. There are few undiscovered secrets in the realm of science, and those will be ferreted out by persistence, following known paths.

'The only room for genius these days, for a breakthrough into unknown lands by a flash of brilliant inspiration, is in the field of biology. There are still many secrets in the processes of life; many problems to which we still must learn the questions before we can hope to discover the answers. Doctors and biologists are the men at the frontiers of knowledge.'

Dr. Moran spoke convincingly, but the words sounded more like a set speech, ready for delivery to any interested lecture group, than the intensely held belief of a sincerely dedicated man. Nancy couldn't have said why she felt this, but she did. He went on to speak of names like Jenner and Murchison, E. J. Marey and Iliya Metchnikoff, and of concepts like the ontological notion of inflammation, and chemotaxis, and metabolic disorders. Nancy found it all interesting; but when he started talking about his own work, she found that she was unable to follow what he was saying. From the look of interest on her brother's face, she was unable to tell whether he was being polite, or was still fascinated by the doctor's conversation.

'But I bore you,' Dr. Moran said suddenly.

Nancy's attention snapped back to the conversation. 'No, no,' she assured him. 'Not at all. I find it fascinating.'

'Then you are tired,' Dr. Moran said. 'Of course, how thoughtless of me. You are both still convalescent. And it is getting late. What you both need is a good night's sleep, and I am going to assure that you get it. Now where did I put my black bag? A doctor without his medical bag is an offense against nature.'

'I feel fine,' Nancy protested.

'Nonsense,' Dr. Moran declared. 'If a doctor were to allow a patient to decide how he felt, where would we all be? Ah, here's the bag.' He fished around in the many compartments in his bag, and then turned to the maid. 'Jane, would you please fetch a pitcher of water. Now then, here it is. Just a mild hypnotic. Sleep is nature's healer, and nature is still far better at healing than any doctor.'

'I *am* feeling a little tired,' Robert admitted.

'You shouldn't be trying to do too much for the first few days out of bed,' Dr. Moran said. He stirred the powder into two glasses of water. 'Here — drink this, each of you, and go to bed. You'll feel refreshed in the morning.'

Robert smiled and toasted the doctor. 'Your health, sir. I suppose you know best.'

'It's my business. A doctor must know best even when he doesn't know anything at all. But in this case, I'm *sure* it's for the best.' He chuckled. 'Believe me, a good night's sleep will be the best thing for you tonight.'

'I do. Come on, drink up, Nancy, and we'll go to bed.'

Nancy resigned herself to not having a chance to speak to her brother before morning. The doctor was probably right: her hip and shoulder were bothering her, starting to tighten up. A good sleep was probably what she needed.

The mild hypnotic must have been pretty powerful; it was quite effective. Nancy spent no time in bed staring at the darkened ceiling going over her growing list of questions and problems. No sooner had she pulled the blanket up around her, feeling the smooth coolness of the sandwiching sheets, than her eyes fluttered closed and she fell into a deep sleep.

The dream — somehow she knew it was a dream — had a sense of urgency and importance. She was in a hallway made up of doors, and she was running from one to the next, opening them and peering inside. The same figure was behind each of the doors: a man in ermine robes wearing a coronet and sitting on a throne. He smiled and turned to her as she opened the door, but she couldn't quite make out his face. She would slam the door and run on to the next one, where the scene would be repeated. Then she saw that her dream-king had Alan DeWit's face. He came toward her with his arms outstretched, but she slammed the door in his face and ran on.

Then the hall had no more doors and she was running down it toward the end, where an unidentified man waited. But the harder she ran, the further away the end — and the waiting man — got. Then she sat down, and for some reason the man was now approaching; but before he reached her, Nancy was suddenly falling and falling — and she awoke.

It was morning. She lay in bed for a while, staring at the bright play of sunlight and shadow in her room and thinking. She remembered most of the detail of the dream, and was sure it had an important meaning for her, if she could only determine what. The trouble with dream interpretation was that it allowed for too many possibilities: a state of mind; a state of the body (a bit of underdone potato, Dickens had suggested); a subconscious resolution and assembly of facts; a reading into the future; a warning, a threat; even a projection of someone else's troubles. And she could do without someone else's troubles. She had quite enough of her own, thank you.

Dreams were often so very vague, as well. Why couldn't they just come right out and say what it was they were trying to convey? Why all this business about faceless men and long corridors? After reviewing three or four possible meanings for her dream, each of them wilder than the dream itself, Nancy decided that the smartest thing would be to forget it and let her future work itself out without aid from the dream world.

And today — today she would tell Robert about Benjamin House and the strange things connected with it. She would tell him what she had discovered, and of her beliefs and suspicions and fears. And he would either take her seriously, at least to the extent of investigating himself, or he would laugh at her and tell her she had too much imagination. He would laugh gently, but it would still hurt. Still, there was nothing more to do now: she must tell him.

She dressed carefully and went down to breakfast. Robert, she found out, had a tray sent up to his room. She ate slowly, marshalling her thoughts; deciding what to tell Robert, in what order, like the captain of a debating team preparing his arguments. After breakfast she went up to his room, to find him sitting up in bed with a plum-colored smoking jacket on, going over a file of what looked to be legal papers.

'Welcome,' he said, waving her to the chair by his bed. 'Good morning, dear sister. I hope you slept well. Dr. Moran was right: a good night's sleep was excellent for my system.'

'I'm glad,' Nancy said. 'Robert, may I talk to you?'

'Of course.' He looked at her for a moment and then put aside the file of papers. 'Has something happened?'

'No. Well, I mean yes, but not . . . Oh Robert, I don't know what I mean!' She pressed her fists against her knees. This was no way to begin, but she couldn't help it. All her ordered thoughts had fled from her head.

'Take your time,' her brother said, looking at her worriedly. 'Is it something you didn't tell us about, ah, the other night?'

'What?' For a second Nancy didn't know what Robert meant. Then she realized. 'Oh. No. It's far more important than that.'

Robert was now clearly puzzled. 'Go on,' he said.

'Well . . . Listen, Robert — have you given any thought to your accident?'

'My accident?' He was still puzzled. 'You mean that damned stone that nearly killed me? I suppose I've thought how lucky I was not to be killed. What do you mean?'

'Supposing . . . ' Nancy took a deep breath. 'Supposing it wasn't an accident?'

Robert picked up a pencil and twisted it between his fingers. 'Go on,' he said.

Nancy told him of finding the ledge from which the stone had fallen, and her opinion that it must have been pushed. She told of seeing a man by the window moments before; a man whom she was certain was Alan DeWit's man, William. That she thought she had seen Alan there a few seconds before that. She told of William's following her to the wax museum, and mentioned how strange it was that he should just happen to be in the street when she had the unfortunate experience with Lord Bryce. The story poured out as she talked: her strange meetings with Alan in the darkened hall and on the roof in the rain. Her finding of the old book, with the penciled map inside. And finally of going down to the cellar and sub-cellar with Gayle, and their finding the freshly oiled gate with traces of digging behind.

When she was finished, she looked at Robert and he looked at her. 'Very strange,' he said finally.

'Then you believe me?' She asked.

'I believe that the things you say happened did indeed happen. However, I'm not sure I agree with your interpretation that Lord Alan DeWit is a villain and a scoundrel and intends to murder us in our beds.'

'But what else is there to think?'

Robert pondered this in silence for a minute, then said, 'I want to examine this ledge where you found the stone; or, let us say, the gap.'

'I'll show you.'

'Fine. I'll get dressed. Wait for me in your room. Here, take a cup of coffee in with you. I'll only be a minute.'

Shortly, Robert — looking elegant and casual and certainly recovered from his encounter with the force of gravity — followed Nancy upstairs into the deserted hallway. 'We seem to be alone,' he said.

'These are all storerooms,' Nancy told him. 'The servants are in the other wing; at least their rooms are.'

'Migod,' Robert exclaimed when they entered the room at the end of the hall-way. 'Look at all the muskets. We could arm a company of guards. A small, obsolete company it would be: I believe these are the famous 'Brown Bess' muskets that were standard issue in the British army until sixty or seventy years ago.'

'I thought they were older than that,' Nancy said.

'They could be. They were used for over a hundred years. Look at these two; they've been cleaned and oiled. Quite recently. I'll bet they could be fired.'

'I forgot to mention them,' Nancy said. 'I noticed them when I came up here before.'

'A pretty little mystery. Probably the last baron went in for shooting muzzle-loaders. We'll ask. Is that the window?'

'That is the window,' Nancy agreed. 'Be careful!'

Robert had swung it open and was leaning out as far as he could. 'Interesting,' he called, pushing himself up on the sill and leaning even further.

'Robert! You'll fall off!' Nancy exclaimed.

'Hold my feet, will you?' Robert said, pushing himself even further out.

Nancy wrapped her arms around his feet and leaned on them. 'What are you looking for? Do you have to go that far out?'

'Wait a second,' Robert called, wriggling slightly further. 'There. Curious, very curious.' He was leaning all the way over, with his nose almost in the gap caused by the missing stone. 'Who would have thought . . . Well, all right, help me get back in.'

Nancy pulled at his feet, and Robert pushed himself up and back inside the window. 'Sometimes I agree with Prudence,' Nancy said. 'You haven't aged a bit since you were ten years old. Did you find anything?'

'You were right,' Robert said, 'and you were wrong.'

'What do you mean?'

He dusted himself off. 'I think I shall need a bath. You're right, as that's where the stone fell from. And you're wrong, as it wasn't pushed from this window. At least I don't think so.'

'Then how did it fall?'

'It didn't fall. It was pushed.'

'Then — '

'There's some sort of mechanism set into the stonework. If you like, I'll lower you down and you can see for yourself.'

'No, thank you,' Nancy said. 'I'll take your word for it. What sort of mechanism?'

'Well . . . come along, let's get back downstairs. I feel like I've been rolling in dust.'

'There's a big spot on your nose,' Nancy told him, taking her handkerchief out and rubbing it away. 'There, that's better.'

'I couldn't see much,' Robert told her as they went back downstairs. 'But there's some sort of iron rod set into a hole in the stone. It's sort of in a groove, and it moves back and forth. The stone below is cut so that the missing one was resting only on two points.'

'What does all that mean?' Nancy asked.

'I think there's some sort of mechanical device hidden somewhere in the house that's connected to that pushrod by a series of levers, so that somebody in another part of the house could push the stone over by merely pushing or pulling a concealed rod.'

'Whatever would something like that exist for?'

'I imagine that when the house was built, the original baron was preparing for unwelcome guests. It must have been built in at that time. Perhaps there are other charming surprises hidden about the house; we shall have to check on that.'

'Then it could have been anyone.'

'Who released the stone? Yes,' Robert agreed. 'At least, we won't know who it could have been until we locate the hidden pull. But you're right: someone tried to kill me. And it must have been just because I am the new baron; no one here could have any personal reason to dislike me.'

'Isn't 'dislike' a rather mild word?'

'Yes, I suppose it is. But how could anyone here hate me? It must be a madman.'

'And it could be any of the servants,' Nancy said, 'or Dr. Moran, or Sir Andrew . . .'

'They were outside,' Robert reminded her. 'It could even still be Alan DeWit or William. The thing we'll have to do is locate the hidden device.'

'How do you go about locating a hidden device?'

'There must be old plans of the house. I mean, besides the cellar. That's probably where our madman found them. I can't imagine that someone would go around tapping walls and twisting bezels and pushing panels on the off-hope that he'll find something.'

'He might if he was looking for a treasure.'

'A point,' Robert said, 'a definite point.' He went back into his room deep in thought.

Nancy had attained her goal, but it had left her somewhere other than where she expected to be. She had told Robert of her findings and fears, and he had believed her. But he had also eliminated her one suspect. Now Nancy again did not know whom to trust or believe. Only one madman — or a conspiracy of madmen? What were they after? Was it the treasure supposedly hidden behind the Benjamin rhyme? And was it only her brother's life that was threatened, or hers as well?

Slowly Nancy went downstairs, planning — or trying to plan — what to do.

Someone else might have decided that it was Robert's worry, now that he'd been apprised of things, but she could not do that. She desperately needed to know what was happening around her, and who was causing it. She thought of the servants. The only one she knew at all besides Meb — and it couldn't be Meb — was Fenton. He was always the correct and proper butler, but what was going on behind that stony face? Did he feel so much resentment toward the new baron that it had driven him mad? Or was it one of the others; the anonymous faces that waited on her and drove her about London? How could she tell which? Could they all be working together in a sinister conspiracy?

Furthermore, why was William following her about? Was he doing it without Alan DeWit's knowledge? Was he, perhaps, trying to protect her rather than harm her? But, protect her from what? Alan must know. Why didn't he tell her? Was it simply a case of that infuriating masculine smugness that assumed that a woman was too delicate to even hear of the seamy side of life, and thus made her more easily a victim of it? How, how could Nancy find out?

Alan was in the front parlor when she entered it, sitting at a desk with his jacket hung over the chair, writing in a large notebook. He started to rise and don his jacket when she came in, but she waved him back to his seat. 'Don't trouble yourself, Mr. DeWit. Please continue what you were doing.'

'I had just about finished,' Alan told her, turning to scribble a few more quick lines and then closing the book. 'It's good to see you this morning, Miss Nancy. How are you feeling?'

'Oh,' she said, rubbing her shoulder, 'an occasional slight ache, nothing more. I am quite recovered, thank you.'

'I'm glad. I was worried.' He smiled. 'You do have such a propensity for falling out of things. You need someone around to take care of you.'

There it was: the masculine conceit. Of course Alan wouldn't tell her anything — she was just a woman, to be put up in a tower where the little splashes of mud wouldn't soil the hem of her garment. 'I'm quite capable of taking care of myself, thank you,' she said coldly.

'Here now,' Alan said in confusion — the first time she had ever seen him so. 'I didn't mean . . . I only meant . . . '

'I know what you meant, Mr. DeWit. If it weren't for you sneaking about, perhaps I wouldn't fall down quite so often.'

'Well, I . . . You . . . Look here, Miss Nancy — we seem to have got off on the wrong foot this morning.'

'The foot I keep tripping on, perhaps,' she suggested.

'There, you see?' he said earnestly. 'What have I done to earn your displeasure? Perhaps we should start in again and avoid the, ah, pitfall.' He turned completely around in the chair until he was looking at her from the other side. 'Ah, Miss Nancy,' he said. 'How good of you to join me. My, but you look radiantly beautiful this morning. But then, of course, you could never fail to look beautiful. 'Beautiful as sweet! And young as beautiful! And soft as young! And gay as soft! And innocent as gay.''

'Another quote?' Nancy said, trying to look stern, but feeling that somehow she wasn't quite succeeding.

'I warned you. Edward Young, about two hundred years ago. I feel safer with other men's lines. I give less away about myself; true emotions and the like. Besides, the ancients have said these things far better than I can ever hope to.

'My last delight! tell them that they
   are dull,
And bid them own that thou art
   beautiful.''

'That's Shelley,' Nancy said. ''Epipsychidion'.'

'Intelligent as well as beautiful,' Alan said.

'If I could write the beauty of your
   eyes
And in fresh numbers number all
   your graces,
The age to come would say, 'This
   poet lies;
Such heavenly touches ne'er touch'd

earthly faces.''

'Keats?' Nancy guessed.
'No,' Alan said. 'A different sort of romantic. That's from one of Shakespeare's sonnets. But Keats knew you too:

'I met a lady in the meads
Full beautiful, a faery's child;
Her hair was long, her foot was light,
And her eyes were wild.''

'Mr. DeWit,' Nancy said, feeling that she might be blushing, 'you'd better stop, or I'll begin to think you're serious.'
'You're right, Miss Nancy,' Alan said. 'We couldn't have that.'
'You must have memorized a lot of love poetry and recited it to a lot of young ladies.'
Now it was Alan's turn to blush, although he didn't seem to be aware that he was. 'I assure you, Miss Nancy, I memorize poetry for my own amusement only. Not much of it is what you call love poetry, and that which is I do not make a practice of reciting to young ladies.'

He seemed quite put out, and Nancy regretted her words. 'What sort of poetry do you recite to, er, other people?' she asked.

Alan paused to consider. 'Kipling,' he said, 'and Fitzgerald.'

'Kipling? You mean like 'Boots, boots, boots, boots', or 'Gunga Din'?'

'That's right,' Alan said, smiling again. 'I recite 'Boots, boots, boots, boots' in quite a dashing manner.'

'I'm sure,' Nancy said, unable to suppress a chuckle. 'Who is Fitzgerald?'

'He translated *The Rubiayat*. Quatrain verses of a Persian poet and mathematician named Omar Khayyam:

'Oh threats of Hell and Hopes of
    Paradise!
One thing at least is certain — this
    Life flies;
One thing is certain and the rest is
    Lies;
The Flower that once has blown for
    ever dies.''

Nancy shuddered. 'Very cheerful,' she said.

Alan continued:

'‘Strange is it not? that of the myri-
ads who
Before us pass'd the door of Dark-
ness through,
Not one returns to tell us of the
Road,
Which to discover we must travel
too.’

'I find that it has a certain fascination,'
Alan said.

'It's very beautiful,' Nancy agreed, 'but
is it all like that?'

'You mean sad and morbid? No, not at
all. Some of it is quite cheerful. I just
happen to prefer these parts.'

'I understand,' Nancy said, thinking
that she didn't understand Alan at all.
She was beginning to hope rather strongly
that he wasn't the one to blame for all her
troubles.

'Ah, there you are,' Robert said,
appearing in the doorway. 'Alan, I wonder
if I could have a talk with you for a few
minutes?'

'Certainly, Lord Benjamin,' Alan said, getting up. Nancy noticed that he suddenly looked worried. The two men paused, and Nancy realized that she wasn't intended to hear the conversation. More masculine presumption.

'I'll leave the room,' she offered.

'No, no,' Robert said. 'That won't be necessary. Alan and I will just go into the den for a few minutes.' And the two of them went through to the next room, carefully closing the door behind them.

Nancy decided that she resented being shut out of the conversation. She went to the door and put her ear to the panel, but was unable to hear more than the murmur of voices. Then she noticed Alan's notebook on the desk. Without knowing what she expected to find, she went over and picked it up. It was bound in plain brown leather, with lined pages stitched in. She flipped through them. The back section was names and addresses. The rest of the book possessed no discernible order or pattern, being a jumble of scrawled notes and figures to be translated, and in some cases transliterated, only by the person who had written them. Able to make nothing out of this, she put the book back carefully, making sure it was just as she had found it.

Having gone this far, Nancy gathered her courage and went one step further. She bent down and went through the pockets of the jacket Alan had left hanging over the back of the chair. As she did this she glanced around, as though expecting to find someone hiding behind the furniture watching her. *I am clearly too nervous to be a good thief,* she thought.

In the jacket, distributed among the pockets so as to create the least possible bulge in the line of the jacket, were the following items: a billfold containing calling cards and paper money, a fine tooled-leather cigar case, a gold cigar cutter, a quill toothpick in a small gold case, a wooden box of wax vestas, and a sealskin tobacco pouch. None of the items could be considered in any way strange, dangerous, or conspiratorial. Nancy put each object back into the pocket where she had found it.

The leather cigar case was in the inside breast pocket, and as Nancy replaced it she felt a piece of paper that she had not seen before. It had been crumpled into the bottom of the pocket, probably by the replacement of the cigar case at an earlier time. She withdrew it from the pocket, opened it, and smoothed it out.

It was a stiff rag paper of fine quality, cut to notepaper size. The letterhead, in firm, no-nonsense bold lettering, read: The Blades 41 Hornblower Court.

Below the letterhead was a note, neatly centered and written in a fine copperplate script, clearly the work of a professional clerk:

To Lord Alan DeWit.

My lord,

As we have notified your lordship in our communication of the 1st inst., we beg to inform you that your account-of-hand now stands at the figure of twenty thousand pounds: £20,000. Please communicate to us your desires as to the rendering of this account, as we wish to clear our books.

Thanking your lordship for your kind attention.

I remain,
Your Humble and Obedient Servant,
Sebastian Tombs
General Manager.

Nancy read this letter through, then she read it again more slowly. Then she folded it back up and thrust it back into the jacket pocket, and sat down in a chair to consider.

Twenty thousand pounds. That was an awful lot of money. She wondered exactly how much gambling it took to lose such a sum — over a hundred thousand dollars. A month? A year? How did Alan, if indeed he was cut off from his family as she had heard, ever intend to repay this debt? Could he be hoping — or expecting — to find the Benjamin treasure hidden away in the cellar?

She returned to the door end pressed her ear to it. She could hear the voices, but was quite unable to make out what was being said. Now she was determined to find out. But how could she manage it without being seen? Nancy had never considered the methods of eavesdropping before, but she had read of it being done in novels. A glass tumbler placed to the door was one way, she remembered. She looked around for a glass, but there were none in the room. The heroines of the books she had read never had to put up with efficient servants. She wouldn't have known which way to place it against the door anyway, although she supposed that a minimum of experimentation would have established that.

The window! If she went outside and stood by it, which she could do without arousing notice with a minimum of care, she would be able to hear everything that went on inside.

She started to go upstairs for her wrap, then realized that by the time she returned the conversation would probably be over, so she just dashed out the front door, leaving it carefully unlatched so that she could get back in without having to ring.

A thick hedge grew alongside the house, so she was unable to get as close as she would like; but as luck would have it, the window to the den was half-open. She went over and started earnestly examining the hedge under it. *If someone comes along,* she thought, feeling foolish, *I shall pluck a few of these leaves and walk off muttering something about leaf-blight.*

The voices came clearly through the window. 'Then it's settled,' her brother said.

'That's the way we'll do it,' Alan agreed. 'You'll have to be careful.'

Be careful? Why would Robert have to be careful? Nancy moved a bit closer.

'When do you expect it?' Robert asked.

The wind rustled through the hedge, and Nancy shivered.

'Tonight,' Alan replied.

12

There are times all the variegated facets of existence combine to one bright, intense point. So Nancy's life seemed to be coming to a focus at a point of time some hours ahead of her, during the coming night. It was clear that something was going to happen then; something that she felt would concern her deeply, although no one wished to discuss it in her presence.

The rest of the day passed quickly: Madame Fortuno sent a carefully wrapped package containing several dresses to her, with a note saying she should try them on for style and then come back to the shop with them for a final fitting. Sir Andrew Dean came over to tell them that their agent in Boston had what seemed a fair offer for the farm. The news seemed to depress Robert. This would be the final cutting-off of the past. He told Sir Andrew that he would have to think about it, although it was certainly the logical thing to do. He had no desire to become an absentee land-lord, which would be necessary if they were to keep the farm.

Then, late in the afternoon, Lady Gayle dropped by for a brief visit. She was brimming with solutions to the cellar mystery, the mildest of which involved a pirates' den, and the most elaborate including a secret tunnel under the English Channel. Nancy found it hard to tell when Gayle was serious and when she was indulging in what she called 'romance'.

At dinner that evening, Robert was unusually quiet and Prudence was completely silent. Nancy tried to start a conversation several times, but found that she couldn't think of anything to say. The meal got gloomier as it went on.

After dinner Robert suggested to Nancy that they play draughts, a favorite evening's occupation with them since they were children. They retired to the study, set up the board and began to play. Robert spent a long time between moves, his shoulders hunched over, puffing on his pipe and staring at the board; but Nancy could tell that he wasn't concentrating on the game. Whatever he was seeing as he stared down at the red and white squares, it wasn't the checker-men.

Dr. Moran marched into the room later in the evening, followed by Alice, who brought a pot of hot chocolate at his instructions. He perfunctorily examined brother and sister, pulling down Nancy's lower eyelid and staring into her eye, and thumping Robert on the skull with his knuckle; then pronounced them fit. 'Rest,' he said, 'that's what does it. There are more miracles in a good night's sleep than in all of modern medicine.' He poured two cups of cocoa and spilled a quantity of white powder in each, then stirred them well and handed one to Robert and one to Nancy.

'One more good night's sleep,' he said, 'and I won't even have to examine you any more. I wish all my patients responded as well to the cure of nature.'

Tonight Nancy did not want a good night's sleep. Whatever was going to happen, she wanted to be awake and aware. The question was, how did one gracefully get out of drinking a proffered cup of drugged cocoa?

Robert yawned and picked up his cup. 'I concede the game,' he said. 'For some reason I don't seem able to concentrate tonight. I think I'll take the hot chocolate up to my bedside table and read in bed for a while before I go to sleep.'

'Splendid,' Dr. Moran said, following Robert to the door. 'Reading in bed relaxes the body and the mind. I strongly recommend it.'

'If it's a sufficiently dull book,' Robert said, smiling. 'Goodnight, Nancy.'

'Sleep well,' she said. As her brother disappeared through the door, and while Dr. Moran's back was still turned, she quickly opened the top of the silver pitcher and poured the cocoa back inside, then set her cup neatly back in the saucer.

'Well,' she said as Dr. Moran turned back, 'I think perhaps I should retire to my room also. It is getting late.'

'Make sure you . . . Oh, I see you did drink your hot chocolate. That's good.' Dr. Moran smiled a tight smile and rubbed his hands together as though he were congratulating himself. 'Good patient; fine patient; splendid patient. I also shall retire to my room, although I'm afraid that some experiments I have to complete will keep me up far into the night. The path of science is a hard one, but it leads forward — and that, after all, is the important thing.'

Nancy wondered what to reply to that, trying to decide between 'that's good' and 'that's too bad'. It all depended, she decided, upon what he thought he was saying. She temporized. 'I hope it works out well,' she said, getting up.

'It will, it will,' he assured her. 'It had better. After all the work I've put into this, ah, project, I had better be rewarded with an answer.'

'It depends, or so I've been told, upon whether you have asked the right question — isn't that so, Doctor?'

Dr. Moran eyed Nancy strangely as she walked to the door. 'That is certainly true, young lady,' he said. 'And very perceptive of you to have said it.'

'Good night, Doctor.'

'Good night, Miss Nancy.'

So Dr. Moran was going to be up tonight too. Nancy had a picture of this large house with small groups of people in different corners of it doing strange and mysterious things. She went upstairs to her bedroom and decided to change into a house dress instead of a nightgown. If anything did happen, she was determined to investigate it, and she didn't want to be impeded by improper garb.

What was going to happen tonight, and how were her brother and Alan DeWit involved in it? And why were they keeping it a secret from her? Perhaps Alan had told Robert some story to lure him away. Then she would find Robert lying on the floor downstairs tomorrow morning, victim of another mysterious 'accident'.

Nancy lay down on top of the covers with a book she had brought with her from the United States: Mark Twain's *Life on the Mississippi*. She determined to try to read until she heard her brother leave his room; then she would follow him and find out what was happening. Supposing he left the premises? She would be unable to follow him then. But somehow she didn't think that whatever was happening would occur away from Benjamin House.

Nancy suddenly realized that she probably wouldn't hear Robert leaving his room if she kept her door closed. Since she was further down the hall than he, Robert probably wouldn't notice if she opened her door, so she quietly turned the handle and swung it halfway open, so that the bulk of the door hid the glare from her bedside lamp. Then she returned to her bed and the world of the riverboat pilots.

An hour passed and nothing happened. There was no sound from either above or below. Nancy's eyes grew heavy, and she had to struggle to keep them open. She regretted not having had the forethought to bring a pot of tea upstairs with her. She sat up on the bed with her legs tucked under her, to make it harder for her to accidentally fall asleep. She thought of moving to the armchair across the room, but she would have to move the lamp to continue reading, and it would shine directly into the hall.

Another hour passed, even more slowly than the first. Nancy crept into the hall once when she thought she heard a sound, but nothing moved and she could hear nothing further. She was well into the book by now, and it was fascinating; but her head felt heavy, and it would be so nice to lie down for just a minute. Of course she couldn't do that; couldn't take a chance of falling asleep. Perhaps if she just shifted to a more comfortable position . . .

What was that? Nancy jumped up at a sudden sound, and realized that she'd been asleep. How long? She looked at the clock on her nightstand: just about two hours lying there with the book on her breast and her legs under her. She flexed her legs, glad to discover that they hadn't gone to sleep in that cramped position.

There was the sound again: a sort of dull, muffled, faraway thump. Nancy put the book aside and got out of bed, then tiptoed down to her brother's room. There was no light from under the door, and she could hear no sound within the room. Cautiously and lightly she knocked; there was no answer. She opened the door to find that Robert was not inside, and his bed had not been slept in, or even sat on, since it was made that morning. Had he slipped out while she was asleep, or had he perhaps never returned to his room at all that evening? That had not occurred to Nancy before, and she bit her lip for not thinking of it.

Where had he gone, upstairs or down? She still felt strongly that he hadn't gone out. Was he perhaps up on the roof, joining Alan in whatever game they had among the chimney-pots? At least tonight it wasn't raining. Or was he downstairs in the cellar, investigating the sinister locked corridor? From what direction had the sound she had heard come? It had seemed to come from all around her, as though the whole house were reverberating to the thump of a giant mallet.

Nancy decided to go downstairs, and she did so slowly, checking all the doors she passed to see if anyone were within. There was no further sound, all the rooms were empty, and all the lights were out save only the dim gas night-lights in the long hallway and on the staircase.

She checked the main floor, but the study was empty, the sitting room deserted, the library still and dark. The kitchen and butler's pantry and all the other rooms were free of human habitation.

She stopped before the cellar door and stood for a while, listening and thinking, with her heart beating fast and a cold feeling on the back of her neck. It was closed and no light showed beneath the jamb, and it led into the cold, dark cellar, and she couldn't take a light because it would give her away, and she didn't want to go down there — she wanted to go back to bed and close the door and pick up her book and forget about what was happening between the cold stone walls of the cellar of Benjamin House.

But Robert might be down there, and the answer to all the questions about Benjamin House and the mysterious events since their arrival might be with him. Nancy put her hand on the knob and slowly turned it, then pulled the door toward her. A cold breeze came up from the cellar with a thin whistling sound and tugged at her dress. The door itself moaned as she pulled it open. And from somewhere below there sounded a faint clatter that brought with it the echoes of the many stone-walled rooms it had passed through before reaching her ears.

At that instant Nancy came very close to slamming the door and running upstairs, but instead she took a deep breath and walked through the doorway. The blackness was complete. When she closed the door behind her all vision stopped.

Slowly and cautiously, with her hand tightly wrapped around the bannister railing, she made her way down the stairway. Each step was a deliberate act of will, harder to accomplish than the last. *This is silly,* she kept telling herself, knowing that it wasn't. *There's no one down here,* she thought. *Surely if there were, they'd have a light. My brother must be upstairs — or out.* But she knew that Robert wasn't upstairs, and she knew that he hadn't gone out, and she knew that the light — for surely there must be a light — was still one flight down in the ancient dungeon beneath the cellars of Benjamin House.

She reached the bottom of the stairs and groped across to the far wall of the corridor with her hands seeking in front of her. *Yes, here is the wall — cold stone and rough — and along this way — yes, here is the first door; this must be the box room.* Directions got so strangely twisted in the dark. This couldn't be the side corridor that led to the larder? No, that would have to be further down.

Nancy walked along with one hand touching the wall and the other extended in front of her to ward off any unknown obstacle that might have appeared since she was here before. She placed each foot carefully in front of her so as to not make any noise. After a minute of walking in this strained position, her mind began to play tricks on her. It seemed as though her foot had come all the way down, and there was no floor beneath. She would have to force her foot down the extra inch to meet with the floor, which she knew was really perfectly level. And the wall seemed to be curving away to the right, although she knew the corridor to be straight.

Suddenly there was another thump: a curious sort of belching sound, still muffled and distant-sounding, but much clearer and closer than last time. The corridor seemed to shake with it, and a layer of dust shook free and billowed into the air, falling on her face and hands and assaulting her nostrils. Nancy fought the sneeze she felt coming and finally mastered it with no more than a few sniffs. She was definitely closer to the sound — some sort of explosion? — and thence definitely closer to where her brother must be. She hurried on as fast as her blindness would let her.

There was a noise in front of her, much softer than the last, but continuous. Nancy paused to make out what it was. Footsteps! And now there was a dim light visible at the end of the corridor, just a faint glow but increasing even as she watched. For a second she couldn't figure out what it was — her light-starved eyes made it seem too impossibly bright — but then she knew. It was the reflection of a lantern. Someone was coming up the stairs!

Nancy flattened herself against the corner of a doorway, her heart beating furiously high in her chest. She tried the door, which was unlocked but very stiff. The creak of the unoiled hinges would certainly give her away if she tried to open it. The footsteps were now at the top of the stairs, and the lantern-light flooded the corridor. There was no chance for her to move now — nowhere to go without being seen. She would just have to pray that whoever it was walked by without peering into any of the recessed doorways.

'Gar! I've 'bout had enough of this blasted dirt.'

'Right enough. I didn't sign on for this to become no blasted miner, nor a mole neither!'

There were two of them! Nancy pushed back into the corner, not daring to look out as they approached. She had never heard either of the voices before. Who could they be, and what were they doing in the cellar of Benjamin House?

'My nose is running, my eyes is smarting, and my head is aching. I tell you, it damn well better be over and done tonight like the boss says.' One of them blew his nose.

'Trust 'im,' the other said. ''E's paying you, ain't 'e?'

'Not enough, I tell you that. Easy money, 'e calls it. Damn 'ard work, I says!'

'Hello!' They had reached Nancy's hiding-place, and the one with the lantern stopped and stared in at her. He was a weazened little man in grubby worker's coveralls, and his eyes looked like little red dots rimmed with black soot. 'Lookey here, Septimus, what I see.' He had an evil grin on his face as he took a shuffling half-step toward her. Nancy was frozen with fear, and seemed incapable of any motion; unable to utter any sound.

'What's that?' the other asked, peering at the doorway. 'My eyes are so filled with this blasted soot that I can't see a blasted thing.'

'Ah, it's a feast for sore eyes,' the first one said, chuckling. 'A woman, Septimus. We've found ourselves a woman!'

13

The two men gathered around Nancy like a brace of fishermen staring at a golden carp. Neither of them seemed to have any idea of what to do with her. Septimus, who was taller, thicker and younger than his companion, rubbed his eyes and stared, and then rubbed them and stared again, as though he expected this apparition to disappear at the next blink. 'A gorl,' he said finally. ''Tis a gorl.'

'What are you two doing here?' Nancy said in a voice that was not her own: a high, frightened voice that came out against her will.

'Ah!' the short one said, doing a small shuffled jig on the floor. 'What're you doing 'ere, now that's the question. And what are we to do with you, being as you are 'ere an' all? Now that's the question, it is. Down 'ere to steal'm some goodies, perhaps, is it? Sneaking down in the dead of night to make off with some goodies

269

while your master and mistress is asleep, no doubt. No doubt at all. Is there?' he suddenly snapped, grabbing Nancy's chin and twisting her head around.

'Take your filthy hands off me!' Nancy said, pushing him away. 'For your information, I am the mistress of Benjamin House. And you're trespassing, and breaking and entering, and probably several other crimes as well.' Nancy was furious, and her anger overcame her fear. 'Now tell me what you're doing down here and who let you in, and if you touch me again I'll scream and have the whole house down here in a minute!'

'Ah!' the little one repeated. 'You must be Miss Nancy, what we've 'eard tell of. It's good to meet you, Miss Nancy; to make your acquaintance, so to speak. You'll just be coming downstairs with us, Miss Nancy. Yell if you like. Scream your pretty head off if you've a mind to. There's no one who can 'ear you 'cepting us; and while I don't mean to sound unchivalrous, we ain't likely to 'elp you none, now are we? Septimus, you go upstairs now and see if you can find that clobbing iron where the boss said. I'll take the woman downstairs.'

'Right enough,' Septimus said. 'You'n be careful, Miss; it's 'orrible dirty and grubby down there. You don't want to get your frock mussed.'

Nancy looked at him in astonishment, but he appeared to be serious. 'You realize what you're doing?' she said. 'This is kidnapping.'

The small man shrugged. ''Anged if we do an' 'anged if we don't. Go on, Septimus. And you come along with me, Miss Nancy.'

Septimus went off, and the small man stepped aside. 'After you, I'm sure, Miss,' he said. 'Come along there.' Nancy was sure he was right: no one could hear her if she screamed, so she didn't. Instead she walked ahead of him down the corridor.

The small man took her down the stone stairway to the lower cellar, through the great room to the barred passageway at the far side. He was humming something as they went, and occasionally gave a little skip. Nancy found this more frightening than an air of sullen villainy would have been.

The barred gate was standing open, and Nancy was led through it and down the corridor to the right. At the end was a door which looked as though it had recently been chipped from the rock, leading to a large chamber. There were lanterns set into the near wall, which cast a dull light on the room and its occupants.

There were three men in the chamber when Nancy and her captor arrived: two working with shovels clearing a mound of rubble from the far wall, and a third sitting under a lantern with his hands and feet tied.

'I've brought you another guest,' Nancy's captor declared as they entered the room.

The bound man looked up. It was Robert. 'Nancy!' he said. 'How did they get you down here? You should be asleep in bed. I had no idea . . . '

One of the shovelers rested his implement against the wall and turned around. 'Miss Nancy, is it?' he said. 'I thought my sleeping powders were more powerful than that. To what do we owe the pleasure of your company?'

'Doctor Moran!' Nancy gasped. 'You! What are you doing down here?'

'Digging, my dear, digging. I shall discuss it all with you in due time; right now I fear I'm too busy. It is a pity that you had to join us.'

'D-don't hurt her,' the other man said, turning around. 'I'm f-fond of the woman.' It was Lord Bryce. Nancy suddenly felt dizzy.

'What's happening here?' she asked. 'What are you doing?'

'Later, young lady, later,' Dr. Moran said. He gestured to the short man. 'Tie her up. Put her next to her brother. And keep an eye on them; we can't afford to let them get away now.'

'Right,' the short man agreed. He pulled a wicked-looking jackknife from his pocket and cut two lengths of heavy cord from a coil by the door. 'Turn around, miss,' he said, and expertly bound her hands behind her, then wound a couple of turns around her ankles and sat her next to Robert on the floor.

'I'm sorry,' Robert said softly, leaning wearily against the wall. 'There's nothing I can do. Why did you come down here?'

'I followed you,' Nancy said. This was not exactly accurate, but she didn't feel that now was the time for lengthy explanations. 'What's going to happen to us? What does he want down here?'

'Treasure,' Robert said. 'He's been looking for it for three years.'

'We're going to have to blast again,' Dr. Moran announced, standing with his legs apart and his hands on his hips and staring at the wall. Then he wheeled around and looked at Nancy and Robert with the same expression: they were just obstacles to be gone around or through to reach his goal. His eyes were the gleaming but emotionless orbs of a madman.

'That's correct,' he told them. 'Three years. By all rights that treasure's mine, and I'm not going to let anyone stand in my way!'

'What makes you think it's down here?' Nancy asked, meeting his gaze with more assurance than she felt.

'I'd like to know that myself,' Robert said.

Dr. Moran gave a dry, emotionless chuckle. 'You see — you are the so-called heirs to the treasure, and you don't even know where it is.' He walked over to stare down at them, like a schoolteacher about to lecture two naughty children. 'You would call the treasure yours! After all the work and knowledge I've put into finding it, you would take it away from me. By the merest chance that puts it under the cellar of Benjamin House, you would have legal right to a treasure that's been hidden for two hundred and fifty years, even though you are incapable of finding it. My work, my intelligence, my perception; all would count for naught. What would I get — a finder's fee? Would you let me keep some small bauble for myself?

'No — it's all mine, and I shall keep it all. A fair share to my assistants and my, ah, financier; and the rest is mine. Not yours — mine. If it were in a field or under the sea or in some inaccessible mine or crag, would you be able to claim it just because some remote ancestor of yours happened to be the one to place it there — when it wasn't even his to begin with? No! And you won't claim it now. It shall be mine, and I will be rich and I won't have to live in the spare rooms of anyone else's mansion — I shall have my own. Mine! And no American heirs are going to stand in my way.' The color drained from his face as he spoke. When he was finished he was dead white, and he rocked back and forth as he was speaking without seeming to notice it.

He turned away from his lecture and dismissed the prisoners from his mind. 'Where is Septimus?' he asked. 'He must set the charges. This will be the last one, hopefully, and we'll be done. At last, at long last!'

'Back shortly,' the small man said. 'And I, for one, will be blinkin' well glad to get out of 'ere.'

Dr. Moran cocked his head and lifted his bushy eyebrows. 'You're being well paid,' he said.

'Not half! Compared to what you

expect to get out of this. Nothing but day laborers, we are. Night laborers, more properly.'

Dr. Moran thrust his hand into his coverall pocket and produced a small but wicked-looking pistol which he thrust out toward his assistant, his arm as rigid as a yardstick. 'You wish to complain about your wages?' he asked in a deadly calm voice.

The small man stood stock-still, afraid to move, and seemed to grow even smaller. 'Not me, guv'nor,' he said, his voice shaking. 'No complaints from me, s'welp me. Me and my mate, we're content, we are. S'welp me.'

Dr. Moran considered for a minute, then decided he was satisfied. The gun disappeared as fast as it had been brought out, and he went over to inspect the wall.

Lord Bryce, who had been standing watching this with a half-bored, half-amused expression on his face, came over to where Nancy was tied and squatted in front of her like a great toad. Unlike the other's coveralls, he was in evening attire. Sooty, dusty, creased and stained, the trousers no longer pressed, the shirt no longer anything close to white, his garb looked like a beggar's parody of aristocratic dress.

'Why did you come down here?' he said mournfully, patting Nancy's face with a grimy hand. 'I like you.'

Nancy twisted aside. 'Keep away from me,' she said firmly, trying to stay in control of herself. His touch felt to her like the touch of some particularly repellent reptile. To be tied up and helpless with Lord Bryce pawing at her was a form of perdition she was not prepared to endure. 'What are you doing down here?'

Surely he could hear the disgust in her voice; but if so, he ignored it. 'Came down to be in at the kill, don't you know,' he said. 'Bad choice of words, that. I, you see, am Dr. Moran's financier. Not rich at all, you know. Not even what you call well-off. But willing to put out part of what I have in return for a promise of adequate compensation. Tonight we're supposed to arrive at our long-awaited goal, and I insisted upon being present.

Even been doing a spot of digging myself. Anything to help out, don't you know. Going to make us all very rich. I am sorry you came down here tonight. Very sorry. It's such a pity to lose such beauty as yours. I could be very fond of you.'

'What do you mean?' Nancy asked. 'What are you going to do to us?' She felt strangely calm as she anticipated the answer.

'It isn't me, my dear gel, I assure you,' Lord Bryce said. 'I jolly well wouldn't harm you for the world. I had rather something else in mind. But surely you see that Dr. Moran can't let you live?' He nodded his head as though they were discussing the weather. 'It's all quite distressing, don't you know. But there's nothing else he can do, is there?' He leaned forward until Nancy could feel his breath on her face. 'I would like to help you, don't you know. Perhaps I can, if you are nice to me. Why not be nice to me, Miss Nancy? You like me, don't you?'

Nancy tried to move her head away, but he merely drew closer. 'Please, leave me alone,' she pleaded. 'Isn't enough happening without you breathing all over me?'

'Miss Nancy!' Lord Bryce said, grabbing her arms and shaking her back and forth. 'This is no time to play games with me. Social conventions are not for us, you and I. I will help you; I commit myself to it! And you know what my word is worth. Kiss me, Miss Nancy!' He pulled her to him and tried to force her head around to meet his lips.

Suddenly Lord Bryce flew across the room as though propelled by a powerful spring, a startled expression on his face. He skidded to a stop, landed in a sitting position, and then fell over on his back. Nancy didn't understand what had happened until she saw that Robert had twisted around and delivered a powerful kick to Lord Bryce's midsection with his two bound feet.

'Bear up, sis,' Robert whispered to her. 'Things are seldom as bad as they seem. Wait it out.'

Lord Bryce stood up and dusted himself off, a gesture about as effective as trying to spoon away the ocean. He glared at Robert for a minute, took one step toward him, and then thought the better of it and strolled casually over to Dr. Moran.

Nancy tried to understand what Robert had meant. Was it merely talk to bolster her spirits during this ordeal, however it might end; or did he actually have some plan that he was waiting to put into action? What sort of plan could a man who was bound hand and foot hope to effect? And where was Alan DeWit, and how was he involved in this?

Nancy had never thought of Dr. Moran as a villain; he had seemed so earnest. She now saw that the earnestness could be interpreted in a different way. And Lord Bryce was a completely amoral fool who neither realized or cared about the consequences of his actions. She and Robert were in the hands of two madmen, each of whom, in his own way, was quite capable of murder.

Robert saw the worried look she was giving him, and he winked at her and softly started whistling. She recognized the tune, from H.M.S. Pinafore, and then the words came back to her:

'Things are seldom what they seem,
Skim milk masquerades as cream.'

Robert was telling her not to worry; that the situation was not as bad as it looked. Well, it would have to get a lot better before it began to look good; but if Robert could sit there, tied hand and foot, and whistle 'Things are seldom what they seem', she felt a little better.

Septimus entered the room then, with a large cast-iron hook swung over his shoulder, and Dr. Moran and his minions went back to work. Septimus was doing most of the work. He stood back from the wall and surveyed it calmly, ignoring Dr. Moran, who was urging him to hurry up. Then he took a piece of chalk from his pocket and made a series of X-marks around a rectangular section of the wall. When he was satisfied, he picked up a large brace and bit; then, bracing it with his chest against the wall, he started the laborous process of drilling a hole in the solid rock. Nancy could see that the section he had marked out looked different, in color and composition, from the surrounding rock.

Dr. Moran strutted over to them. 'You didn't know, did you?' he said. 'Behind that wall lies the final hidden room, and in it the answer to the Benjamin riddle. And it took me to find it!'

'Come on,' Robert said, 'how do you know there's anything back there?'

'How do I know? How did I know this room was here? Or the corridor? They were both sealed off years ago, and the cement mixed and aged to look like the native stone unless you knew just how to look. Well I was looking for it, and I knew where and how. Two years ago, when I started chipping away at that first wall, I knew of the existence of this room and the room behind. And inside of an hour we'll be through to it, and the Benjamin treasure will be mine.'

'You knew all this two years ago?' Robert asked.

'I did.'

'Then why did you wait so long?'

'I was patient. I didn't want to call any

attention to myself. How was I to know they were going to find an American heir to the Benjamin title? When you moved in I knew I couldn't stay indefinitely, so I had to move quickly.'

'You must have had the stone dropped on me,' Robert said. 'Were you trying to scare me away?'

Dr. Moran leaned over, his dark, expressionless eyes staring into Robert's. 'Lord Benjamin, I released that stone myself. I was trying to kill you!'

'But why?' Nancy gasped. 'Why would you want my brother dead? How could that help you?'

Dr. Moran turned to her. 'I had nothing against your brother, my dear. His identity was immaterial to me. It was the accidental fact that he was the new lord, and would therefore sleep in the master bedroom. Had I had my wits about me then, I would have merely burned the room out, forcing him to sleep elsewhere until it was repaired. But I was rattled. I admit it, I was rattled. I hadn't expected you to come over so fast, you see.'

Nancy tried to make sense of that, but couldn't. 'What was so important about that bedroom?' she asked.

'Of itself, nothing. But for a small accident of design, there would be no problem. You see, that bedroom is the one place in the house where you can hear sounds which emanate from this sub-basement. There is an ancient airshaft right outside this door. It connects with the one behind a grate in the master bedroom. As a result, even the slightest sound made down here can be clearly heard in one corner of the master bedroom. Not loudly, you understand, but clearly. I discovered that when I first started work and the last Baron Benjamin complained of strange thumping noises coming from his wall at night. I was put out, I tell you. His unfortunate demise was quite a relief to me.' Dr. Moran nodded. 'Yes, quite a relief.'

There was a quality in his voice as he said this which made Nancy suspect that Dr. Moran had provided his own relief. If he had murdered the last Baron Benjamin two years ago, he certainly wouldn't hesitate to kill Robert and herself now.

Robert looked up at Dr. Moran as though there was nothing abnormal in the situation, and he were used to having quiet conversations with gentlemen who had tied him up and were planning to kill him. 'You've done an outstanding job,' he said, 'getting all this work done without raising suspicion. It must have been quite a task.'

'It might appear so,' Dr. Moran said smugly, 'but with the proper organization and planning, the most difficult tasks can be achieved with ease. I've had my workers in here opening up the sealed sections of the cellar for two years without discovery. It is really a shame, in a way, that you two had to discover me on the last day. Tonight is the culmination of over two years of effort. I cannot allow your presence to spoil it. Besides, although I have never been inside a gaol, I am convinced that I would dislike the experience. You are definitely an inconvenience to me.'

'How did you deduce that the cellars were here?' Robert asked, for all the world like a gentleman in a club inquiring of the gentleman in the next chair concerning the weather. *How can you be so calm?* Nancy wanted to scream. Then she realized that Robert might have an ulterior motive in keeping the doctor talking.

'That's the most interesting thing,' Dr. Moran said, obviously pleased to tell anyone how clever he had been. 'You see, an ancestor of mine once did a job for an ancestor of yours.'

'Really?'

'Yes. My father's grandfather was a builder. He was hired by Lord Ephriam Hooker, the sixth Baron Benjamin, to find the Benjamin treasure or end once and for all the rumors that there was a treasure to find. He spent six months searching the house, top to bottom, and came up with nothing.'

Nancy remembered that the story was mentioned in the book she had read, but it hadn't mentioned the name of the builder. Not that she would have made the connection if it had.

'If he found nothing,' Robert said, 'how

could his great-grandson suddenly discover the secret almost a hundred years later?'

Dr. Moran smiled a toothy grin. 'Over a hundred years,' he said. 'When I met the old Baron Benjamin — it was in the capacity of a physician, of course; how else could a man of my humble means hope to meet a rich and influential baron? — I recollected that I had come across the name in some old family documents in a chest at home. Purely in a spirit of curiosity, for I knew nothing of the treasure then, I obtained the documents and carefully read through them. I learned of the treasure, and of my great-grandfather's search for it, and came to the same conclusion he had: that if he couldn't find it, it wasn't there.

'Then I made my great discovery.' Here Dr. Moran paused for effect, nodding his head like a chicken. 'On such little threads is greatness born. There was a leather portfolio containing the surviving original plans dealing with the construction of Benjamin House — plans spanning a period of almost two centuries. My great-grandfather must have simply neglected to return them to the Benjamin library, since he had no earthly reason to keep them. He was utterly convinced that there was no Benjamin treasure.

'As a doctor I was trained to be thorough. I read through the plans and I examined the portfolio. There, on the inside of the portfolio, firmly affixed to the leather side as though it had been glued in place, was an ancient sheet of paper. It was not fastened there deliberately, as far as I could tell. I must assume that constant dampness at one period had affected the glue in the very fiber of the paper and caused it to become so fastened.

'I carefully steamed the paper loose and removed it from the portfolio. It turned out to be the original rendering of this cellar we are standing in. By comparing it with my ancestor's chart of the same, I quickly ascertained that the cellar had a corridor and three rooms that no longer appeared on the map. No wonder my great-grandfather had been unable to locate the treasure. Measuring wall thicknesses and thumping for hollow spaces will not locate a walled-up area in a stone cellar; not if it has been cleverly done.' Dr. Moran pulled a thick black cigar from his inside pocket, bit off the end, and lighted it, puffing clouds of acrid smoke into the already dust-filled room.

'Now that I was sure that there was a treasure,' he continued, 'I went about making friends with the late baron. Within a reasonable length of time, I found myself living under his roof as a semi-permanent guest. I had the function of taking care of the failing health of the old man, which I did faithfully while I began my exploration of the cellars of Benjamin House. My only mistake was with that ventilating shaft, but you see the old baron was deaf. It wasn't until he passed on, and his son moved into that bedroom, that the sound was noticed. Pity about that.'

'Why did it take you this long to get the job done?' Robert asked.

'Get it done? You don't understand. Up until quite recently I was doing it all myself. Spending the day taking care of the old lord, and the night digging. The old map wasn't too accurate about directions, and there are several areas of the cellar wall that are reinforced with concrete. I dug several holes that led only to solid rock before I found the right one. Then, when I found the chamber and was convinced I was right, I enlisted the aid of Lord Bryce. With his help, and his money, things were speeded up considerably.'

Septimus had finished drilling the holes, and he now filled them with what looked like long black candles.

'Get up,' Dr. Moran directed Robert and Nancy. 'We are going to blow out the last plug remaining between me and the treasure, and I wouldn't want you to be hurt in the explosion.' He lifted Nancy up as if she were a sack of rice and carried her to the small outer chamber, setting her against the wall by the far door. He and Lord Bryce assisted her hobbled brother to a place right next to her. 'You just stay there,' he said.

'It doesn't look like I'm going very far,' Robert said wryly.

Septimus came out of the room. 'All

set,' he said. 'Have any of you gentlemen a match?'

Dr. Moran fished a pack of wax vestas out of his coveralls and flipped them to Septimus, who saluted. 'Thank you,' he said. 'Stay out of there now; I'm going to light the fuse. 'Bout a minute burning, if I figure right; but them things are undependable. Be right back.' He disappeared into the room.

Someone was whistling 'Greensleeves'. It was a strange and out-of-place thing to hear in the dank stone room. The tune reverberated from the walls, and seemed to come from all directions. Nancy looked around. It was no one in the room with her. Septimus? It seemed unlikely.

Now she could hear footsteps along with the whistling. Someone was coming down the stone corridor toward the room. Dr. Moran heard it, and he turned around, a surprised expression on his face.

The footsteps stopped, and Alan DeWit stood in the doorway. His elegant evening dress and gold-tipped cane looked proper on him, even in the depths of the earth. 'Evening, all,' he said, tipping his hat.

Septimus came from the inner room. 'Any time now,' he said, then he saw Alan in the doorway and froze, looking surprised.

'Another one!' Dr. Moran snarled, and reached into his pocket.

'Now, now,' Alan said, and his cane whipped through the air. It connected with Dr. Moran's hand just as he pulled out the gun, sending it skittering harmlessly across the room. Lord Bryce, coming out of his trance, reached for it, but Alan took two quick steps across the room and calmly stepped on his hand.

Then, suddenly, came a deafening blast from the next room, which shook the ground and sent a wind of hot air through the door.

'It's open!' Dr. Moran yelled, forgetting about everything else. 'We're through!' He raced back through the doorway.

There was a curious rumbling sound in the wake of the blast. Septimus cocked his head and listened. 'I've heard that before,' he said. 'In the mines. If it's what

I think it is . . . '

'The treasure!' Lord Bryce said. 'I've got to see what I paid for.' He stalked after Dr. Moran.

'What is it?' Alan asked, looking at Septimus as the rumbling intensified.

'Water, sir,' Septimus said. 'Underground spring or such, breaking through under pressure. We've got to get out of here — quick!'

'Then let's go!' Alan said. He twisted the handle of his cane and pulled out a slim knife. 'Here, Nancy, turn around,' he said, kneeling and starting to slice through the ropes around her ankles.

'No argument, sir,' Septimus's little companion said, pulling out an enormous jackknife and sawing at Robert's bonds. 'You'll remember that I helped?'

'We'll discuss terms later,' Alan said. He pulled Nancy to her feet. 'Are you all right? Can you walk?'

'Yes,' she said.

'Good. Let's get out of here.' The five of them ran through the door and down the corridor. The rumbling grew louder, and then there was a cracking sound and a wall of water assaulted the door they had just come through. A stream raced down the corridor ahead of them, and in a few seconds ice-cold water foamed around their ankles. Suddenly the lantern went out.

'Take my hand,' Alan yelled over the roar of the water, and clutched for Nancy's hand. He pulled her down the corridor with relentless strength, through water that was now over her knees.

A sudden surge of water broke Alan's grip, and Nancy fell and was swept forward into the icy stream. She tried to regain her footing, but the floor kept slipping beneath her, and the rocks bruised and cut her as the current slammed her against the wall. The icy water was numbing, and she couldn't think: the tremendous roaring seemed to come from inside her own head. She fought to breathe, but couldn't find the surface. *Goodbye*, she thought, and everything went grey, and nothing mattered, and she was floating . . .

A hand touched her, then grabbed for her; then an arm was securely around her waist, lifting her head out of the water. 'Nancy, are you all right? Nancy?'

'What? S'right,' she said, and sagged in his arms.

There was a sharp stinging, and then another. Nancy opened her eyes. She couldn't see anything, but someone was slapping her face and calling: 'Nancy! Nancy! Wake up!' It was Alan. How curious. He seemed to be crying. 'I can't carry you out of here,' he yelled into her ear. 'The current is too strong; it would wash us both away. Nancy! You've got to wake up!'

Finally something got through to her, and she shook her head. 'Stop hitting me,' she said. 'I'm — I think I'm okay now. Let me rest.'

'No rest,' Alan yelled. 'I don't know how high the water's going to get. We must get out of here.'

The water was now over her waist, and still rising. 'Come on,' Alan said, holding her firmly around the waist.

'Where are we?'

'In the main chamber. The stairway is somewhere ahead of us. Come on!'

They made their way as rapidly as possible in the rising water until they had crossed the room and were up against a stone wall. 'I hope this is the right wall,' Alan said. 'We may have been turned around by the current. The stairs should be somewhere to our right.'

Suddenly a light appeared about five feet to the right. A second later a lantern, and the man holding it, came into view down the stairs. It was Fenton, in a full-length night-shirt and stocking cap. Right next to him was Robert.

'Thank God,' Robert said. 'Let me help you.' He waded into the water and helped pull Nancy and Alan out.

'How did you get here so fast?' Alan asked, sitting wearily on the step.

'I tripped,' Robert said, 'and the water pulled me right to the steps. I was just going up for a light when I met Fenton here coming down.'

'I thought I heard a noise,' Fenton explained. Alan broke out laughing.

'May I inquire as to what has occurred — or is occurring?' Fenton asked.

'Later,' Alan said. 'First — there are

some more people down here, and I suppose we might as well try to save them.'

'I'll take Nancy up to bed,' Robert said, 'and be right down to help.'

'I'm all right,' Nancy insisted, but she allowed herself to be led upstairs. Robert woke up Prudence, who must have undressed Nancy and put her to bed, because she woke up the next morning in a dry nightgown and warmly in bed; but Nancy couldn't remember.

14

Septimus was found and saved. Robert decided not to turn him over to the police, and he gratefully disappeared into the night. No trace was ever found of Dr. Moran, or Lord Bryce, or the third unnamed member of the band. The waters continued filling up the cellar until there was no more to fill; then they stopped.

'I'm glad you're not a villain,' Nancy told Alan the next day over cups of tea in the parlor.

'So am I,' Alan said, smiling. 'Did you think I was?'

'She was convinced you were responsible for all the mysterious happenings at Benjamin House,' Robert said.

'Oh. I am sorry about that.'

'Well you were certainly acting strangely,' Nancy said. 'What about that night in the ballroom — or on the roof?'

'Believe it or not, that night in the ballroom I was practicing darts. I do things like that; always have. Uncontrollable. On the roof I was listening in on the plans of Dr. Moran.'

'You were? Was he up there too?'

'No, he was down in the basement. But there's a ventilation pipe that runs right up to the roof, and if you put your ear to it . . . '

'Oh. But what about the note?'

'What note?'

Nancy put her fist to her mouth. 'I shouldn't have said that. You had a note in your jacket, and I read it. It said you owed twenty thousand pounds to some club.'

'Reading my notes?' Alan said, with a fierce scowl. Nancy was a second realizing he was only pretending. 'Well, if you're going to, you should read them properly. *They* owe *me* the money, not the other way around.'

'Well!' Robert said. 'You can make that kind of money gambling?'

'You can if you're one of the owners of the club. Four friends and I founded The Blades a few years back, and it's done very well. That's why I had to leave home;

my father disapproves. Not of gambling, you understand, but of owning a club. He thinks it smacks of being a tradesman.'

'Isn't gambling illegal here?' Robert asked.

Alan sighed. 'It depends on the day of the week, the temperament of the judge you ask, the moral indignation of the populace, and a thousand other things. The statutes are so vaguely written that it's hard to tell, In general the way The Blades conducts its business — scrupulous honesty and all that sort of thing — is considered acceptable.'

'All secrets are coming out today,' Robert said.

'Except the 'secret of Benjamin Square',' Nancy said. 'Now I suppose we'll never know.'

'If the treasure was down there,' Robert said, 'we'll never find it now.'

'It wasn't!' Alan said. He leaned back and grinned at the effect he created. 'No, I'm not pulling your leg. The treasure trove of Charles the First is in this house at this very minute, and not under twenty feet of water either.'

'I suppose you know where it is,' Nancy said. She had meant to sound scoffing, but it came out as a flat statement. She wouldn't be surprised if Alan did know where it was.

'I do,' he confirmed.

'Well,' Robert said, getting up, 'waste no more time, man. This I must see!'

'It's all a matter of interpretation,' Alan said, leading them into the ballroom. 'Remember, Nancy, I told you about the live chess games?'

She nodded.

'Well, I was thinking about that one day last week, and then I thought of the rhyme, and it all fell into place. Benjamin Square is the square on the board Lord Benjamin played on when the king was playing.'

'Which square is that?' Robert asked.

'Think of your coat of arms.'

Robert snapped his fingers. 'A rook!'

'Correct. And which rook? The king's, of course.' Alan walked over to the square in the great marble floor.

'What about pacing out the steps?' Nancy asked.

'The next line tells us how,' Alan said. 'Left march when? 'When you come about the great ring.''

'What great ring?' Nancy asked, searching the floor for anything that resembled a ring.

'The bishop's, of course,' Alan said.

'Of course,' Robert agreed. 'Bishops wear rings, don't they? Kind of a seal of office.'

'Kind of,' Alan agreed. He marched to the bishop's square from the rook's and did an abrupt left face. 'That,' he said, pointing to the white square directly in front of him, 'is the place. There the Benjamin Treasure has reposed for — how long now? — two hundred fifty years.'

'You sound as sure as Dr. Moran,' Robert said.

'Surer. I've seen it.' Alan took a slim knife from his pocket and slid the blade along the crack in the stone. 'It's like a Chinese puzzle-box,' he said. 'The stone has now lifted ever so slightly up. If you walk on it, it will reset, and you'll never notice it. But if you push gently out

303

. . . up . . . and now to the left, if I can get it . . . there!' There was a click, and the stone slid smoothly up, until it was about three inches above the remaining squares. Alan grabbed one side and pulled, and it swung up on silent hinges. 'Beautifully made,' he said. 'Look inside, my lord. The trust of the Benjamins is intact.'

Robert and Nancy both went over and looked down. There, in the dark interior of this secret place, rested a small ornate chest. It had been there, undisturbed, for over two hundred years. 'Can we lift it?' Robert asked.

'A fortune in jewelry is not all that heavy,' Alan said. 'If you'd help me . . . '

Robert took the other side of the chest, and they pulled it up. Alan undid the clasps. 'It's not locked,' he said. 'Your ancestor must have decided that if anyone found the chest, no lock was going to deter him from opening it.'

Inside the chest was a tightly packed collection of small and large wooden boxes containing linen-wrapped pendants and rings, scepters and coronets: the baubles and symbols of a kingdom.

'They're beautiful!' Nancy said, picking up a heavy gold ring with a great inset emerald to examine. 'They look like they were put away just yesterday.'

'Gold doesn't tarnish,' Alan explained. 'And gems don't age.'

'This will go back to the Crown,' Robert said decisively.

'Of course,' Alan agreed. 'The queen will be delighted to accept it in the name of her ancestors and descendants, and the people of England. These jewels will probably end up in the Tower of London.'

'They were up here all the time,' Nancy said. 'Then I wonder why those rooms Dr. Moran found were blocked off.'

'He read the wrong books,' Alan said. 'He should have read the histories of your family instead of his own.'

'Do you know?' Nancy asked.

'There's a reference in an old family bible,' Alan told her. 'You'll find it in the library.'

'In a bible? What sort of reference?'

'In the page for family history — births, deaths, marriages and the like. In the year sixteen sixty-five, after three people died in three days, is the note: 'blocked off ancient cistern.''

'That was a cistern? But why the note in the bible?'

'Those three people died of the plague. Sixteen sixty-five was the year of the great plague in London. It was generally believed that the plague was caused by bad vapors rising from polluted water. So, when three people in his household were carried off in one day, the Baron had the cistern, and the rooms leading to it, cemented off.'

'And two hundred years is sufficient time for the cistern to fill many times over,' Robert said. 'It must be part of an underground stream to hold so much water.'

Nancy noticed that Alan was looking at her with a new sort of interest now, and she thought she liked it. Benjamin house was going to be a happy place in which to live, now that she knew that the sounds she might hear in the night would be friendly.

'Miss Nancy,' Fenton said, appearing in the doorway, completely unperturbed by the box of treasure opened at his feet, 'Lady Gayle has arrived.'

'Tell her I'll be right out,' Nancy said. 'Ask her to sit down — I have a story to tell her!'

We do hope that you have enjoyed reading this large print book.

Did you know that all of our titles are available for purchase?

We publish a wide range of high quality large print books including:
Romances, Mysteries, Classics
General Fiction
Non Fiction and Westerns

Special interest titles available in large print are:
The Little Oxford Dictionary
Music Book, Song Book
Hymn Book, Service Book

Also available from us courtesy of Oxford University Press:
Young Readers' Dictionary
(large print edition)
Young Readers' Thesaurus
(large print edition)

For further information or a free brochure, please contact us at:
Ulverscroft Large Print Books Ltd.,
The Green, Bradgate Road, Anstey,
Leicester, LE7 7FU, England.
Tel: (00 44) **0116 236 4325**
Fax: (00 44) **0116 234 0205**

Other titles in the
Linford Mystery Library:

DEATH DIMENSION

Denis Hughes

When airline pilot Robert Varden's plane is wrecked in a thunderstorm, he goes to bail out. As he claws his way through the escape hatch, he is struck by lightning and his consciousness fades into oblivion. Miraculously, Varden cheats death, and awakes in hospital after doctors succeed in saving his life. But he emerges into an unfamiliar world that is on the brink of devastating war, and where his friends are mysteriously seventeen years older than he remembered them . . .

MRS. WATSON AND THE DEATH CULT

Michael Mallory

When the body of a prominent businessman is found floating in an ancient Roman bath, all the evidence points to a young man named Ronald Standish as the murderer. His wife appeals to her old governess Amelia, the second wife of Dr. John H. Watson, for help. Soon, Amelia is thrust into a baffling mystery involving the practice of ancient pagan religious rites in the modern city of Bath. At every step, though, she finds evidence that makes the case against Standish even stronger . . .

THE LORD HAVE MERCY

Shelly Smith

The married life of Robert Mansbridge and his wife Editha is the talk of the village. Whispers of infidelity and wantonness abound; whilst most of their neighbours respect the doctor, Editha is regarded as a shrew. Meanwhile, timid Catherine Duncton is hopelessly in love with Robert, but chained to her invalid father; and sculptor Leslie Crispin carries a torch for Editha. Then Editha dies in mysterious circumstances, and the rumour mill churns ever faster and more fiercely . . .

THE NEXT TO DIE

Gerald Verner

When a body is found under a pile of gravel at the foot of a bank, it looks as if the storm the previous night blew a cart-load over just as the man was passing underneath. But amateur criminologist Trevor Lowe notices that the soles of the dead man's shoes are caked with cigarette ash: clearly he never walked to the gravel site, but was carried there. It is the first of a whole series of murders. Can Lowe unmask the criminal — or will he be the next to die?